THE WIND
BLOWS DEATH

Titles by Cyril Hare:

DEATH IS NO SPORTSMAN

DEATH WALKS THE WOODS

AN ENGLISH MURDER

TENANT FOR DEATH

TRAGEDY AT LAW

UNTIMELY DEATH

THE WIND BLOWS DEATH

WITH A BARE BODKIN

THE WIND BLOWS DEATH

CYRIL HARE

HarperPerennial

A Division of HarperCollins*Publishers*

To
Arnold Goldsbrough

Contents

1. PLANNING A PROGRAM   1
2. EXEUNT SEVERALLY   13
3. THE EVE OF THE CONCERT   23
4. THE REHEARSAL   33
5. IN SEARCH OF A CLARINETIST   44
6. A CONCERT INTERRUPTED   53
7. INTRODUCING TRIMBLE   60
8. JENKINSON   71
9. INTERVIEW WITH AN ABSENTEE ORGANIST   82
10. INTERVIEW WITH A BEREAVED HUSBAND   93
11. A CONFERENCE WITH THE CHIEF   103
12. LUNCH AT THE CLUB   115
13. POLISH INTERLUDE   124
14. BLUEBOTTLE'S PROGRESS   133
15. PETTIGREW UNBOSOMS HIMSELF   146
16. SELECT DANCE   155
17. THE TRUTH ABOUT VENTRY   165
18. THE TRUTH ABOUT K.504   177

19. MADAM HOW AND LADY WHY   188

20. *DA CAPO*   199

1

Planning a Program

In his time Francis Pettigrew had aspired to, and even applied for, a number of appointments of different kinds. He had in fact held not a few, most of them honorary. But the last job that he had ever expected to come his way was that of honorary treasurer to the Markshire Orchestral Society.

It was, he reflected as he sat in Mrs. Basset's overfurnished drawing room, one of the many unexpected things that he owed to his marriage—itself perhaps the most unexpected event in his career. As a middle-aged bachelor, marrying for love a woman young enough to be his own daughter, he had been philosophically prepared for a good many surprises, and he had certainly had them. Possibly the greatest had been the ease with which he had accomplished the transition to a life of domesticity in the country after so many years bounded by the Temple, the circuit and the club. For this the break in his professional life occasioned by the war was, he recognized, largely responsible. It had always been a remote and distant dream of his one day to retire to some pleasant spot on the Southern Circuit within comfortable reach of London, there to indulge in a genteel and strictly localized practice until such time as the stanchest clients should write him off as

1

hopelessly senile; but the chains of habit had been too strong, and the prospect of loneliness had appalled him. But when, at the end of hostilities, he thankfully escaped from the trammels of Government service, the proposition suddenly seemed quite feasible after all. Hitler had left the Temple with barely half its buildings and less than half its charm; the difficulties of resuming his London work seemed, to a man who had been consistently overworking for four years, insurmountable; and he was no longer alone in the world. Furthermore, he candidly admitted, the money which Eleanor brought with her made the prospect of retirement, alleviated by such pickings as the circuit might afford, considerably more attractive. Now, two years later, he was able to regard with detached amusement the unspoken but obvious conviction of his cronies on circuit that he must be miserably unhappy.

All the same, he told himself as he looked round the room, he had not bargained for this. It had begun innocently enough, when Eleanor had confessed to a passion for music. Pettigrew had raised no objection. He had a liking for music himself, though through laziness and pressure of other interests he had done little to cultivate it. Next it appeared that she not only enjoyed listening, but herself could play the fiddle passably well. So far, so good. No reasonable husband could object, particularly when this blameless occupation was coupled with an undertaking, scrupulously carried out, to practice only when he was out of the house. From that it followed logically enough that within a few months of their settling in Markhampton she should establish herself among the second violins of the county orchestral society. The trouble really began when he allowed himself to be called in, quite unofficially, to advise the committee over an absurd quadrangular dispute in which the society had involved itself with the Markhampton City Council (as lessors of the City Hall), the Commissioners of Inland Revenue (who were interested in the collection of Entertainment Tax) and the Performing Rights Society. He did not find it very hard to compose the difficulties, but in an unguarded moment he let fall the opinion that they would never

2

have arisen if the accounts of the society had been kept in a more orthodox manner. From that moment he was a doomed man. It was in vain that he protested that he knew nothing of bookkeeping, that his personal accounts were in a disgraceful state of confusion. He had unwittingly acquired the reputation of a sound, practical man of affairs, and there was no escaping it. Remorseless pressure was brought to bear upon him from every side, and when he learned that Mrs. Basset, who led not only the orchestra's cellos but also an important section of Markhampton society, was making Eleanor's life a burden on the subject, he capitulated. And here he was, perched uncomfortably on one of Mrs. Basset's hard, shiny sofas, dutifully attending a committee meeting.

"I call on the secretary," said Mrs. Basset in her high, neighing voice, "to read the minutes of the last meeting."

Robert Dixon was the secretary—a middle-sized man in his early forties, with smooth dark hair and a smooth face that was so utterly undistinguished as to make Pettigrew perpetually uncertain whether he would recognize him again, often as he might meet him. Dixon's presence on the committee had somewhat puzzled him at first. He was, for one thing, obviously not a music lover in the sense that the other members were. Indeed, he appeared to treat the whole business of concert giving with an easygoing contempt that only just stopped short of being offensive. But it was certainly a contempt born of familiarity, Pettigrew observed; for along with a complete indifference to music as such, went a surprisingly intimate knowledge of the mechanics of music treated as a business. Agents and their terms, the idiosyncrasies of soloists and the lowest fees they would be likely to accept—matters of this order were at his finger tips. It was all most useful, and, in view of his attitude to the subject matter, extremely aggravating. Pettigrew had often wondered how Mrs. Basset put up with him.

Enlightenment had come when something let fall by Mrs. Basset had sent him to the Markshire County Library to consult *Debrett*. Research there had established the fact that Dixon was the

3

great-grandson of a viscount. That explained everything. For in the armor plate with which that angular, elderly lady confronted and imposed upon the world there were two weaknesses, and two only. One of them was snobbery—a snobbery, moreover, of a rare and delicate variety. She did not merely, as the grosser type of snob will do, love a lord; she reveled in the faintest tincture of blue blood, the remotest connection with the humblest title, and she had an uncanny gift for tracing them. It was she, and not Eleanor, who had disclosed to Pettigrew that his wife's maternal great-uncle had been a baronet, and she had done so with the happy air of one conferring some rich gift. Indeed, Pettigrew formed the view that she took a collector's pride in nosing out whiffs of aristocracy in unlikely places, and that she would prefer the joy of meeting the second cousin of a peer of her own discovery to the more obvious thrill of being introduced to a duke. On the other hand, he had never seen Mrs. Basset being introduced to a duke and he could not be sure.

"Mr. Pettigrew! We are waiting for the treasurer's report."

Guiltily recalled from his daydreaming, Pettigrew hastened to present his accounts. They had been previously subjected to a private and searching audit from Eleanor, so they had no difficulty in passing the scrutiny of the committee. This duty discharged, he had intended to slip away, for a glance at the agenda had shown that his presence at the rest of the meeting would be purely decorative. But a glance through the open door of Mrs. Basset's dining room had shown a promising assortment of refreshments for those who stayed the course, and there was besides a certain pleasure to be gained merely from sitting there and observing the inhabitants of the strange world in which he now found himself. He decided to remain.

"Programs for the season's concerts," announced Mrs. Basset importantly. "Mr. Evans"—her hard visage softened perceptibly—"what suggestions have you for us?"

If the aristocracy was one of Mrs. Basset's weaknesses, Clayton Evans, the creator and conductor of the orchestra, was the other.

4

She worshiped him with an uncritical adoration that in anyone less formidable would have been ridiculous. For his sake she worked like a slave in the interests of the society, cajoling troops of her reluctant friends to subscribe to its funds, visiting with her wrath any playing member who missed a rehearsal. For his sake she endured long hours of practice until by sheer determination she had made herself into a very passable cellist. His slightest wish was her law, a word of approval from him would send her into ecstasies. Above all, she made it her mission in life to stand between her idol and any outside annoyance, and this she performed with terrible efficiency.

In all fairness, Pettigrew thought, one had to concede that Evans was a worthier object of adoration than widows in middle life are apt to find. He was an impressive figure as he sat in an armchair in the center of the group, his domed, bald head sunk on his chest, his long legs thrust out in front of him, peering myopically from side to side through the enormously thick lenses of his spectacles. Exactly how near Evans was to complete blindness was a matter of speculation among members of the orchestra. It seemed fairly certain that his vision from the rostrum did not extend beyond the first two desks of the strings, and his habit of cutting friends dead in the street was proverbial. On the other hand, he appeared to be able to read music with uncanny ease, though to what extent he in fact relied upon a phenomenal memory rather than on the score before him was open to doubt. Since the orchestra seldom ventured on modern works the matter was not easily put to the test. The important point was that Evans was by training and temperament a musician of a high order. Debarred by his disability from a career elsewhere, he devoted himself to the musical life of the county. The inhabitants of Markshire, as was to be expected, rewarded him by taking him very much for granted, and expressed surprise when visitors from outside commented on their good fortune in possessing such a distinguished resident.

Evans drew some papers from a pocket of his baggy suit and held them close to his nose.

"I take it that we shall give our usual four concerts this season," he said in his thin, clear voice. "Two before and two after Christmas?"

There was a general murmur of agreement.

"I have provisionally booked the City Hall for the first Thursday in November," said Dixon. "That should suit for the first concert."

"Very well. I take it further that our subscribers will expect something in the way of a concerto at each of them?"

"You'll never get people to come without one," observed Miss Porteous with a sigh. She was a plump, rosy young woman, an excellent violinist, but perennially and unreasonably pessimistic about everything.

"Yes, we want a draw," Evans went on in a resigned tone. "I was going to suggest a fiddle for the first concert—say Lucy Carless. She tells me she will be back in England by then."

The name of Lucy Carless, which was familiar to Pettigrew from concert advertisements, met with almost unanimous approval. The one person who hesitated to agree was, unexpectedly enough, Mrs. Basset. She pursed her lips, raised her eyebrows and then leaned across towards Dixon. Pettigrew, who was sitting next him, caught the quick exchange of words without in the least understanding them.

"You're quite sure you wouldn't mind, Mr. Dixon?"

"Mind? Me? I couldn't Carless!"

"Lucy Carless!" said Mrs. Basset, a shade too emphatically, turning to Evans. "That will be delightful! And what is she to play?"

"Oh, the Beethoven, Mr. Evans!" yearned Miss Porteous. "Please let it be the Beethoven!"

"Steady on!" broke in the rich voice of Mr. Ventry from a far corner of the room. "We had the Beethoven only the year before last. There *are* other composers, y'know."

Evans paid no attention to either disputant. "We are a bit overdue for the Mendelssohn centenary," he observed, "but better late

6

than never. Lucy really plays the Mendelssohn concerto quite passably. We'll try that."

"I wonder if people want to hear Mendelssohn nowadays," Miss Porteous began doubtfully, but Mrs. Basset cut her short.

"Nonsense, Susan. If they don't like it, they ought to. And they'll come to hear Lucy Carless, anyway."

"The Mendelssohn won't take it out of her too much," Evans went on, "so I shall ask her to play a group of solos after the interval. That will mean one less work for the orchestra to rehearse—and I don't intend us to be underrehearsed this season if I can help it."

"Oh, quite, quite!" Mrs. Basset breathed her earnest agreement.

"It'll mean paying for an accompanist, too," Miss Porteous pointed out.

"That shouldn't be a large item," Evans observed. "I don't know who accompanies for her now."

"Lawrence Sefton," answered Dixon promptly. "He ought to be cheap enough. She never paid him much and now she pays him nothing. She married him last year," he explained. The fact seemed to cause him saturnine amusement.

"So much for that," Evans went on. "Then to finish up with, I propose we should do the Mozart Prague Symphony."

"Oh, the Prague!" said Mrs. Roberts (viola), speaking for the first time. "That's the one that goes da-di-*da*-da, pom-pom, isn't it?"

"No," answered Evans, kindly. "It isn't. But it's very nice all the same, and well within our scope." Taking the meeting's approval for granted, he went on: "All we want now is a shortish piece to open with." He paused and peered towards the corner of the room. "Ventry, I believe you had a suggestion to make?"

Ventry cleared his throat and answered without hesitation, "Well, yes, as a matter of fact, I had. I thought it was about time we gave old Handel a break. There's a ripping piece by him, I had in mind—it's an organ concerto as a matter of fact—you'll know it, of course, Evans, but I expect it'll be new to the rest of you. The Alleluia, it's called."

7

"The Hallelujah Chorus?" asked Mrs. Roberts brightly.

"Oh, Lord, no! Nothing to do with that. It's in B flat, the second book. I forget the op. number—"

"Opus 7, number 3," said Evans.

"That's the chap. Two short movements, and plays for about twelve minutes, so it would be just about right for a curtain raiser. I've always wanted to have a stab at it on the City Hall organ— splendid instrument—so if you could see your way to put it in the program, I, for one, would be grateful."

"I'm sure you would, Mr. Ventry," said Miss Porteous, rather acidly.

"Mind you," Ventry hastened to assure her, "it's got a simply corking part for the orchestra. Really, that was what I had in mind when I suggested it. I thought we could do it with Henry Wood's scoring, if you agreed, Evans—with clarinets. Adds a bit of color to it."

"By all means," said Evans. "That is, if the rest of the committee agree. Personally, I think the Alleluia concerto would suit our purposes very well."

Mrs. Basset, rather pink in the face, echoed him. "I am sure we are all greatly obliged to Mr. Ventry," she said. "It sounds a most delightful piece."

"Oh, it is, Mrs. Basset, I assure you. You'll love playing it."

To an outsider, Evan's deference towards Ventry in the matter of Handel's Alleluia organ concerto was in odd contrast to the autocracy he had displayed with regard to the rest of the program; but Pettigrew knew enough of the affairs of the society to appreciate the little comedy that had just been staged. Ventry was a coarse, stout young man with a flair for music and a great deal of money. He owned a large house just outside Markhampton which contained a fine collection of musical instruments and an organ. Pettigrew had been there with his wife and had formed the opinion that Ventry was no more than a mediocre performer, though his enthusiasm for the instrument was beyond dispute, and he was certainly a passionate admirer of Handel. He was sure that, left to himself, Evans would not have selected Ventry as a soloist at one of his concerts. For that matter, left to herself, Mrs. Basset would probably not have tolerated him on her committee. Unlike Dixon, he had certainly no hidden aristocratic strain in his pedigree, and he was decidedly not of the type to commend itself to her. But as treasurer to the society Pettigrew was well aware that they had not been left to themselves. For some years past the balance sheets of the society had shown an annual deficit. On each occasion the gap between income and expenditure had been filled by a donation—sometimes quite a considerable one—from an individual invariably referred to by Mrs. Basset as "an anonymous donor." (Many innocents, even on the committee, believed that the generous unknown was Mrs. Basset herself, and she had certainly never troubled to disillusion them.) Now the anonymous donor had decided to come forward and claim his reward. It was as simple as that.

Somewhat dazed, the rest of the committee accepted Clayton Evans's proposal that the concert should open with the piece favored by Ventry, and the program was complete. Pettigrew intercepted something very like a wink from Dixon as he jotted down the items on the minutes. Then Evans became severely technical on details of scoring and the provision of orchestral parts, and the hon. treasurer's attention wandered. It was recalled by an unexpected breeze which blew up over the somewhat esoteric question of the wood wind. Pettigrew, whose knowledge of orchestral music was extremely limited, was vaguely aware that at the back of the orchestra were a number of more or less inconspicuous persons who blew into or through variously shaped instruments, and he was surprised to find that the provision of these presented a problem of difficulty and long standing.

"As usual, we look like being horribly weak in wood wind," Evans remarked. "Fellowes is quite a passable flute, but apart from him there's nobody capable of playing first in any of the instruments, and we simply haven't an oboe at all. It's such a nuisance—it makes the rehearsals so difficult. Dixon, you'll have to

9

engage the professionals as usual. Let's see, that will be two oboes, one clarinet—"

At this point Ventry and Mrs. Roberts began to speak at once. Ventry got in first.

"Young Clarkson isn't at all bad on the old clarinet now," he said. "He's come on a lot lately."

"I know," said Evans. "I'm allowing for him. He can play second to a good first quite capably."

"Young Clarkson," Ventry persisted, "is dead keen to play first this season. He asked me to mention it particularly."

"He's not good enough."

"Young Clarkson says that if he can't play first this season he won't play at all."

"Very well," said Evans curtly. "Arrange for two clarinets, will you, Dixon, please?"

It was apparent from his manner that there was a point beyond which even anonymous donors could not presume on the conductor's tolerance, and Ventry subsided with a flush of annoyance. But the matter was not concluded. Mrs. Roberts had not yet had her say.

"Oh, Mr. Evans," she broke in rather breathlessly, "if it's a question of a clarinet, I've got just the man."

Pettigrew was decidedly fond of Mrs. Roberts. She was an unassuming, good-natured woman, with an untidy mop of gray hair and a perennially worried expression, which usually proved to be due to a kindly preoccupation with somebody else's troubles. She was the wife of a competent, successful man of business, the leading auctioneer in Markhampton, and most unfairly had been allowed by fate to become the mother of a long string of competent, successful children, with the result that her highly developed instinct for helping those weaker than herself had to be satisfied outside the circle of her family. A lame dog had but to look at a stile in Mrs. Roberts's presence to find himself firmly and kindly lifted over to the other side. She had become notorious in this respect, and it was plain from the tightening of the muscles round Evans's jaw that the prospect of a lame dog among his wood winds did not appeal to him any more than young Clarkson had done.

"Really, Mrs. Roberts," he said, "don't you think it will be best if we leave the clarinets in professional hands in the usual way?"

Mrs. Roberts assumed an air of determination entirely foreign to her except where someone else's interests were concerned.

"He *is* a professional," she answered. "That's just the point. At least, he used to be. Just at present he's a Pole."

There was a pause during which the meeting digested this remark, and then Evans, who, like Pettigrew, had a soft spot for Mrs. Roberts, said kindly: "Perhaps you had better tell us all about him, Mrs. Roberts. What is his name, in the first place?"

"Tadyoose—Oh, dear! I never can remember it properly—let alone pronounce it. I've got it written down somewhere."

She fumbled in her bag, and produced a piece of paper, which she passed to Evans. On it was written in block capitals the name Tadeusz Zbartorowski.

"Yes," said Evans, noncommittally, "I see that he's a Pole."

"He is really a most deserving man," Mrs. Roberts insisted. "He can't go back to Poland, he tells me, because of being massacred—if he does go back, I mean. I am most anxious to help him, and I promised—"

"Quite. But what makes you think he can play the clarinet?"

"Oh, he can certainly play—he's playing now in the Silver Swing Dance Band—that's only in the evenings, of course. I *think* he works in the black market when he's not playing—so sad, isn't it? But he'd *much* rather play in a real orchestra, I know."

"I hardly think—" Clayton Evans began.

"He used to play at the Warsaw Opera House before the war," Mrs. Roberts added as an afterthought.

"Oh!…That's put rather a different complexion on the matter. If your friend is everything you say, perhaps we could do something for him." Evans looked at his watch. "It is getting rather late, and we have three more programs to settle yet. Dixon, you

11

have some knowledge of Poland, I think. Perhaps you wouldn't mind seeing this man, and if he is really as well qualified as Mrs. Roberts suggests you could use your own discretion about engaging him."

"I'll put him through it all right," said Dixon, somewhat grimly. "I didn't live five years in Warsaw for nothing."

"Now as to the second concert," Evans went on. "I suggest ..."

At this point the treasurer passed into a deep coma.

2

Exeunt Severally

For Mrs. Basset the high light of the evening came after the meeting had dispersed. Following a custom that had become a convention, Evans remained behind for a few minutes of gossip while he drank a modest brandy and soda, prepared by her own aristocratic hands. It was a delicious interlude of rare intimacy with her idol which she savored to the full.

"Well, Charlotte," he said. "I thought the meeting went off pretty well, didn't you?"

"You managed it beautifully, Clayton. You always do."

Nobody had ever heard Mrs. Basset address him publicly otherwise than as "Mr. Evans" and, since the death of Mr. Basset ten years before, no human being had been known to have the temerity to call her "Charlotte." The surreptitious exchange of Christian names never failed to give her the exciting sense of secret indulgence in a guilty pleasure.

With faintly glowing cheeks she went on: "You don't think there'll be any trouble with Mr. Ventry, do you?"

"Not the slightest, I should imagine. He's really not a bad performer when he gives his mind to it, and the Handel piece is quite within his powers. He deserves a run for his money, I think. We may have a bit of trouble about the tuning of the organ, though. I must speak to the city organist about it."

"I wasn't thinking about that, but about Mr. Clarkson. Mr. Ventry seemed quite upset over him."

"I don't think we need worry about that," said Evans carelessly. "He'll soon forget it. Clarkson is quite impossible, anyway. I shall be glad to be rid of him. Why can't we get anybody to take up these wind instruments *seriously*, I wonder?"

But Mrs. Basset was not, for the moment, interested in wind instruments as such.

"It wasn't like Mr. Ventry to show such anxiety about befriending a *man*," she observed.

Evans laughed. "Well, his reputation doesn't run in that direction, so far as I know," he said. "I'm not well up in these matters myself, but—"

Mrs. Basset pursed her lips.

"There *is* a Mrs. Clarkson, I know," she said, reflectively. "I must make inquiries."

"You think that that may be where Ventry's interest lies? Well, that's certainly the oddest motive I've ever heard for trying to foist a dud onto an orchestra. But aren't you being a bit too imaginative, Charlotte?"

"Perhaps I am, Clayton. But Mr. Ventry is a deep person, I am afraid; very, very *deep*." She shook her head solemnly, and added: "And fond of women. The very opposite of my idea of what a man should be, in fact."

"Quite," said Evans quietly to his glass of brandy. He knew his Charlotte too well to take her more high-flown remarks literally, but the picture she had conjured up of the ideal man who should be a shallow misogynist was a little too much for him. To change the subject, he said: "I hope you approve of the programs."

"Of course I do!" Mrs. Basset breathed loyalty, into which she contrived to put a hint of reproach that her loyalty should ever have been questioned. "I was afraid for a moment that there might be a little awkwardness when the name of Lucy Carless

14

was mentioned, but fortunately it all passed off very well."

"Awkwardness? I know Lucy can be awkward enough sometimes, but why should anyone be awkward about her?"

"Didn't you know that Mr. Dixon had been married to her?" Mrs. Basset asked solemnly.

"Really? I knew Lucy had been married before her present venture, but I never connected her with Dixon. I'm so bad about people, I'm afraid. Are you sure?"

Debrett had materialized in Mrs. Basset's hand, apparently of its own volition.

"Married, first, 1937 (marriage dissolved, 1942), Lucille, only child of Count I. Carlessoff; secondly, 1945, Nicola, eldest daughter of Henry Minch, Esquire," she read. "I wish I could find out who Henry Minch was," she added. "But Mrs. Dixon is very reserved."

"Well, that's Lucy all right," Evans remarked. "She must be the only violinist on record with a foreign name who prefers to play under an English one. She always was a perverse little cuss. But I hope I haven't put my foot in it with Dixon."

"Oh no," Mrs. Basset reassured him. "He is quite unconcerned about it. In fact, he made a little joke about it—I can't remember what it was, but I know it was very witty. People are so *modern* about divorce nowadays, I can't think why. But of course, Mr. Dixon had something more important to think about this evening. Do you think I ought to have congratulated him or not? It is so awkward."

"What on earth are you talking about, Charlotte?" Evans stifled a yawn.

"Didn't you see this evening's paper? I thought you must have noticed."

"I certainly saw the paper, but I didn't observe anything about Dixon in it."

"Lord Simonsbath's only son," said Mrs. Basset portentously, "has been killed in a motor car accident."

"It seems an odd subject for congratulation, at first sight, Charlotte, but I presume that that book in your hands has something to do with it."

Mrs. Basset nodded.

"On the failure of the elder branch," she said, in a hushed tone, "our Mr. Dixon will inherit the peerage."

"Dear me!" said Evans flippantly. "What a disappointment for Lucy. She always had a hankering after titles."

"The matter isn't quite so simple as that," Mrs. Basset went on. "We can't be sure yet whether the elder branch *has* failed."

"Not be sure? With Debrett to go by? I thought that he at least was infallible in such matters."

"I'm not saying a word against Debrett," said Mrs. Basset reprovingly. "Of course not. That's not the point. But the young man who has just died leaves a widow, and the paper says— papers are so crude nowadays—that she is—I prefer to say, in an interesting condition."

"Interesting appears to be the word," Evans yawned openly this time. "I shall look forward to the next installment in this drama in high life. If I were in Dixon's shoes I should pray that it should be a son. I can't imagine anybody wanting to be a lord in these times."

Before Mrs. Basset had had time to recover from this blasphemous observation, he had thanked her for his entertainment and taken his leave.

Meanwhile, the great-grandson of the second, and prospective heir presumptive to the sixth, Viscount Simonsbath was discussing much the same topics with Nicola, eldest daughter of Henry Minch, Esquire.

Nicola was getting ready for bed when Dixon reached home. He found her sitting at her dressing table, brushing her thick auburn hair with slow, languid strokes, as if at any moment she might stop for sheer exhaustion. She was not really tired, he knew, but merely temperamentally incapable of doing anything in a hurry. She had probably been going to bed for the last hour, and she might continue to brush her hair for another ten minutes, merely because it was too much trouble to stop. He sat down quietly on the bed and watched her with a connoisseur's approval. Some day, he reflected sadly, Nicola was going to get fat, if she didn't brisk up a bit and take more exercise; but just at present she was enormously attractive. She had the creamy complexion that sometimes accompanies hair of her particular shade; fine, regular features and particularly beautiful rounded arms. Presently she caught his eye in the looking glass and smiled lazily.

"Well?" she asked, without stopping the slow, rhythmic movement of the hairbrush. "What sort of an evening was it?"

"Much as usual. I've been left to do the donkey-work for the concerts, of course."

"Well, Robert, you know you enjoy doing it, God knows why, so don't complain. Have you fixed up anything interesting?"

"We've fixed up Lucy for the first concert, if you call that interesting," said Dixon.

Nicola laid down her brush and turned round to look at him.

"The hell you have!" she said softly.

"Any objections?"

"Not a bit. It'll be rather interesting to see what she looks like now. Pretty gaunt and scraggy, I should imagine, from the way she was going when we saw her last." She turned back to the glass and contemplated her own pleasing curves with complacence. "Was Billy Ventry at the meeting?" she asked abruptly.

"Oh, very much so. Why do you ask?"

"Nothing…He rang me up just after you had gone this evening."

"What ever for?"

"Well, nominally it was to ask you what time the meeting was fixed for. Actually, it turned out, it was to invite me to come to the pictures with him tomorrow afternoon. I wonder how he found out that you were always kept late at the office on Thursdays?"

17

Dixon laughed dryly.

"That man is the most unblushing womanizer at large," he remarked. "Did you accept?"

"I told him I was going to tea with Mrs. Roberts, which happened to be perfectly true. But it interested me, because presumably it means that his present affair with whoever it is is petering out and he's nosing round for someone else. How do people like Billy manage to get away with it, Robert?"

"Search me," said Dixon, getting up. "Come on, it's time we were in bed."

As he was getting into bed, some twenty minutes later, Robert Dixon remarked: "By the way, you saw the evening paper, I suppose?"

"You left it lying about downstairs," replied Nicola with a yawn, "but the headlines didn't look very interesting, and I hadn't backed anything, so I couldn't be bothered to open it."

"Well, if you had, you'd have seen that my cousin Peregrine's dead. Car smash."

"Good Lord!" Nicola remained silent for some moments. "There's no one else between you and old Simmy, then?"

"That's just the point. There may be. We shan't know for a month or two. Peregrine's widow is expecting."

Nicola began to laugh quietly. "How damn funny!" she remarked.

"I don't see there's anything funny about it. It's a confoundedly embarrassing position for me to be in—for both of us, for that matter."

"Darling, I know it is."

"And old Mother Basset gnashing her teeth at me in agonies of silent excitement only made it worse," Dixon went on.

"She'll gnash still more when she hears about me."

"What on earth are you talking about?"

"Well," said Nicola, "I've got a strong notion I'm on the same tack as Peregrine's widow. I didn't want to tell you till I was quite sure."

18

"Well, well!" said Dixon. He stared at the ceiling in silence for a moment or two and then reached up and switched off the light.

Ventry's house outside Markhampton was a roomy, ugly Victorian place. Ventry would have sold it long before but for the fact that some previous owner had added to it a large, lofty billiard room which, after some ruthless and expensive alterations, served very well to house his organ and an extensive library of music. On returning home from Mrs. Basset's he went straight to this room, poured himself out half a tumbler of neat whisky, lodged it precariously on the music-rest of the organ, and proceeded to play from memory, with great dash and inaccuracy, the C Major Toccata of Bach. It was one of his favorite pieces, both for its own sake and because the long pedal passage with which it opens leaves the performer's hand free to pick up a glass when required. When the whisky and the Toccata were both finished he sat for a moment filled with that exquisite feeling which, before the word acquired a political flavor, was known as "appeasement." The sensation gradually ebbed away as he became conscious of two facts. The first was that his cook had that morning threatened to give notice if her sleep was again disturbed by "noises in the middle of the night"; the other that the telephone was ringing persistently in the hall.

Swearing under his breath, Ventry swung his thick legs off the music stool and went to attend to the more tractable of the two troubles.

"Darling," said a high-pitched voice, as soon as he lifted the receiver, "You've been *ages* answering. Is anything the matter?"

Ventry grunted.

"How did things go at the meeting?"

Ventry was still under the potent influence of whisky and Bach, and for the moment he could think of the meeting only in terms of the City Hall organ.

"Oh, damn well," he replied incautiously. "Really very well indeed."

19

"Then it's all right about Johnny?" said the voice hopefully.

It was on the tip of Ventry's tongue to say, "What about Johnny?" but his brain cleared in time. Distastefully, he conjured up a vision of Johnny Clarkson, with the rabbity teeth and narrow, suspicious eyes.

"Oh, Johnny!" he said. "Well, I'm afraid Evans wasn't inclined to be very helpful so far as Johnny was concerned. In fact, he turned him down flat. I'm awfully sorry, Vi, and I did my best, of course, but there it is."

"Darling, how sickening!" wailed the voice. "Can't just nothing be done about it, not even to please pore little Violet?"

"Not unless he'll come in as second again," answered Ventry shortly. Mrs. Clarkson's kittenish manner, he reflected, sounded its worst over the telephone.

"And that's just what he won't do—he's got a positive thing about it. You know what he is when he's like that. Billy boy, what are we going to do? If he isn't in the orchestra it'll mean he'll be at home every evening, and you know what a suspicious devil he is. We shan't have a chance to see each other."

"I know." Ventry did not sound unduly distressed at the prospect.

"It's only because he's out at his Masonic meeting I've had the chance to ring you up," Violet went on peevishly. "It's like living with a detective in the house, having him around. D'you know, I've been wondering if he hasn't begun to suspect something lately. Can he have found out anything, do you think, Billy boy?"

It was borne in on Ventry with all the force of a sudden revelation that he loathed above all things being called "Billy boy."

As he was pondering this significant fact the voice asked reproachfully, "Haven't you anything to say to comfort your pore little Violet?"

"We've got to be pretty careful, that's all," said Ventry firmly. The idea of being taken in adultery by Johnny Clarkson filled him with nausea. "I think we'd better lie low—not see each other for a bit, and so on."

"Billy boy, you're wanting to get rid of me!"

"Nonsense, Vi, nonsense, but you must understand ..."

It was fully five minutes before he could finally put the receiver down. Upstairs, he could hear shuffling sounds which, he knew, meant that his cook was ostentatiously and revengefully wakeful. He went up to bed heartily cursing the whole race of women; but while he was undressing he contrived to think of two or three exceptions to the general ban.

In the Markhampton Palais de Dance things were just beginning to warm up. A Select Dance, promoted by the Imperial and Antique Community of Bisons, was in progress, and the Silver Swing Band (under the direction of its talented and popular conductor, Syd Smithers) was giving of its best. The din was terrific. The clarinetist, his fingers flying automatically up and down the wooden barrel of his instrument, kept his large, melancholy eyes fixed upon the leader's gyrations and tried in vain to dissociate himself from the hideous noises he was producing. Why, he wondered for the hundredth time that evening, should his instrument be prostituted in this way? The saxophone—of course. The piccolo—perhaps. But why—as the band launched into yet another repetition of that haunting refrain, "Livin' an' Lovin' for Yew" —why the clarinet?

At the first interval he slipped off the platform and made his way to a telephone box at the back of the hall. It was late, but he knew that Mrs. Roberts would excuse him, and he could not wait till the morning for the news he sought.

"Mrs. Roberts? This is Tadeusz Zbartorowski speaking. Forgive me to be so late, but I had to know. Is it arranged for me that I play in your orchestre?...I see. I thank you very much, Mrs. Roberts. And this Mr. Dixon, I see him when?...Good, that will arrange itself, I shall satisfy him. And what do we play?...Oh, you have forgot! That is a pity, but Mr. Dixon will know perhaps....Who, did you say?...Lucy Carless! Well, even for her I don't mind playing now....No, I did not mean that, Mrs. Roberts,

21

but there are things that—no matter, it is a long time ago now....Yes indeed, I am very happy, Mrs. Roberts. I thank you many times. And, Mrs. Roberts, there is a friend of mine who perhaps can find me some nylon stockings if you would let me know your size. ..."

"Well," said Eleanor Pettigrew, "how did you manage at the meeting?"

"Splendidly," yawned her husband. "Splendidly."

"What was settled?"

"Let me see. The anonymous donor is going to have a stab at the City Hall organ, and Dixon couldn't Carless."

"Wretched man! Is that all you learned at the meeting?"

"Absolutely all. Except that Mrs. Basset has some prewar sherry which is not to be despised."

"That," said Eleanor rather coldly, "I had gathered already."

3

The Eve of the Concert

The year advanced; the evenings drew in—not, as in Pettigrew's youth, in decent, ordered gradualness, but with the snap of an elastic band as summertime came to an end and the clocks went back; and the first concert of the season was at hand. The day before the concert was, for Pettigrew, one of acute anxiety, and this for reasons quite unconnected with music as such. The performance was fixed for eight o'clock on Thursday evening, and the rehearsal with soloist and full orchestra (including the professional wind instruments as to which there had been such a pother) for three in the afternoon. At the meeting in Mrs. Basset's drawing room, when the date had been arranged, it had quite escaped his attention that Markhampton Assizes were due to begin at the City Hall on the preceding Monday. To his fellow members on the committee, to whom the course of justice merely meant a few paragraphs in the local paper and a blurred photograph of a bewigged figure emerging from the cathedral, this was a matter of supreme unimportance; but Pettigrew saw in it the possibility of sheer disaster. Four days were normally allotted to the Assize. If the Judge was still sitting on Thursday afternoon, while Ventry was letting himself go on the organ in the same building, there would be a very nasty scene. It was Mr. Justice Perkins, too—a notoriously testy and self-important fellow. Almost equally unpleasant to contemplate would be the reactions of Clayton Evans, his nerves strung to the pitch always produced by a final rehearsal, on being told by an usher or a constable that his lordship required this noise to stop. It did not bear thinking of, but he could not help thinking of it, all the same.

When he was first made aware of the position, by the delivery of two or three briefs, it was already too late to do anything about it. Inquiries from the circuit officials, however, reassured him. The calendar was a short one and the criminal business should be easily disposed of in a couple of days. As to the civil work, there was only one effective action, and he was engaged in it himself. Pettigrew estimated its duration at a day and a half at the most. With anything like luck the Judge should be out of harm's way by midday on Thursday. He decided to say nothing to anybody about his fears but let matters take their course, with a silent vow never to make such a floater again.

Then things began to go wrong. On the Monday, two prisoners who had hitherto disclosed no defense elected to plead "Not Guilty," and two woodenheaded Markshire juries took an unconscionable time to come to perfectly obvious conclusions. This threw the timetable out of gear, but it was still possible for the Judge, by sitting an extra hour in the afternoon, to finish his list on Tuesday. Vain hope! In a fit of geniality as unwonted as it was untimely, Perkins J. acceded to a request to fix the last criminal case for Wednesday morning, for the convenience of counsel. Wednesday morning came, and Perkins dallied lovingly with a perfectly simple case, like a cat with a morsel of fish, while Pettigrew writhed impotently on his seat in the well of the court. With six witnesses on either side and a solid and slow-moving opponent, there was now not the remotest chance of finishing his own case until well into Thursday afternoon.

Pettigrew took stock of the situation during lunch and decided that it called for heroic methods. He was briefed for the defendant

24

and he was reasonably confident that he would succeed on the facts of the case. But there was a slim chance—one that he had never seriously envisaged before—of winning the action on a technical point before any evidence had been called. It was a desperate gamble. The argument would take up most of the afternoon. If it failed—or if Perkins decided, as he well might, to reserve his decision on it until he had heard the witnesses—the orchestral rehearsal was irretrievably ruined. He took the risk, and at the earliest possible moment rose and submitted with every appearance of calm that on the pleadings he had no case to answer.

It was, he realized, a thoroughly unpopular thing to do. The Judge, having reconciled himself to sitting next day, would not like having his arrangements disturbed. Pettigrew's lay client, like all lay clients, would be deeply distrustful of technical points and quite convinced that the facts were all in his favor. His instructing solicitor would naturally disapprove of a course which had never been hinted at in the brief and be seriously worried as to the prospects of getting the witnesses' expenses allowed on taxation, should the case collapse without their being called. He could almost feel the pressure of these unexpressed emotions as he developed his argument, but it was abundant consolation to be aware at the same time that the most perturbed and disgusted man in court was his opponent, whom he had taken completely by surprise.

Spurred on by dire necessity, Pettigrew made his submission with a warmth and earnestness quite unusual to him. Never was a legal quibble argued with such passionate emphasis. His solicitor remarked afterwards that he didn't know Pettigrew had it in him. Neither, for that matter, did Pettigrew. Apt illustrations and analogies flew to his tongue of their own accord; cases he had not looked at for years sprang unbidden to his memory; every forensic weapon came ready to his hand, from ironic jests at the expense of the plaintiff to deep organ notes appealing to the basic principles of the Common Law. It was a performance that could not fail of its effect. Mr. Justice Perkins was dragged against his will from boredom to attention and from attention to eager interest. When Pettigrew at last sat down he looked over his pince-nez to counsel for the plaintiff and said: "What have you to say, Mr. Flack?" And Mr. Flack, for once in his loquacious existence, had very little to say, and nothing to the point. The gamble had succeeded.

Pettigrew reached home about six, triumphant and exhausted.

"How did your case go today?" Eleanor asked him.

"Darling, it was magnificent! I feel exactly like the Dutch boy who stopped the leak with his finger."

"Like a Dutch boy?"

"Not *a* Dutch boy—*the* Dutch boy. You must know the story, surely. There was a hole in the dike, and—"

"Of course I know the story, but what on earth has it got to do with the Assizes?"

"I'll tell you in a minute. But I feel absolutely cooked. I must have a drink before I say another word."

"You'll be having plenty of drinks directly," said Eleanor unsympathetically. "You're not to have one now."

"My dear girl, why on earth not? Are we short of gin or something?"

"As you might have noticed from my clothes, we are going out to a party. We shall have to start now if we're not to be late."

"A party? Are we? Where? You never told me."

"Mr. Ventry," said Eleanor patiently, "invited us two weeks ago to a pre-concert cocktail party. The whole orchestra is coming. I reminded you at breakfast this morning."

"So you did. I'm sorry, I'd forgotten all about it. Sorry I didn't notice your new frock, either. It's charming. Goes well with the hat."

"The frock, as you call it, is nearly two years old. It's the hat that's new. Don't apologize, but I do think you might take a little interest in the concert. The orchestra might just as well not exist so far as you are concerned."

"That," replied her husband in measured tones, "is the greatest

26

injustice I have ever heard perpetrated in my life—and I speak as an expert in these matters. By way of penance, I propose to occupy the time in going to the party by recapitulating all the arguments which I advanced to Perkins J. this afternoon, with special reference to the little Dutch boy and the Markhampton Orchestral Society."

By the time that Pettigrew and a suitably chastened Eleanor reached Ventry's house, the music room, in which the party was held, was already crowded with samples of almost every class in the highly stratified society of Markhampton. Ventry was a man who believed in mixing his guests as well as his drinks. From the door he could just be seen at the far end of the room. He was talking to a tall, striking young woman, whose thin, intense face, framed in masses of dark hair, seemed to Pettigrew faintly familiar. At her elbow was a lanky, red-haired man whom he had certainly not seen before. Pettigrew belonged to a generation that believed in recognizing the existence of one's host, even at the most crowded assembly. With Eleanor at his heels, he plunged into the jostling mob, most of whom, adherents to the modern theory of self-determination for guests, had not bothered to go beyond the bar. Once past this traffic jam the going was comparatively easy. Ventry greeted them with his usual expansiveness.

"Good of you to come all this way!" he exclaimed. "I mean"—he indicated the mass of humanity between himself and the door—"as far as this end of the room. I know a host ought to mingle freely with his guests, like the Royal Family at a garden party, but I'm too fat to get about in crowds. So I stay up here and reward the faithful with a special drink"—here Pettigrew found a large glass pressed into his hand—"and an introduction to a special visitor. Miss Carless, I want you to meet Mr. and Mrs. Pettigrew."

Considering that he had seen her photograph outside the City Hall two or three times a day for the last week, Pettigrew felt somewhat ridiculous at not having recognized her. As to the lanky man with sandy hair, he had been quite right in thinking that his face was strange. He proved to be Mr. Sefton, whom Petti-

27

grew recollected as having been mentioned at the committee meeting as Miss Carless's husband and accompanist. "Accompanist" was the appropriate term in every respect, he thought. While the party lasted he was hardly ever separated from her, and when anybody came between them he followed her continually with his watery, narrow eyes. "Unattractive blighter," thought Pettigrew, as he noted his efforts to show a decent interest in Eleanor's conversation while looking over his shoulder in his wife's direction. Just for the fun of it he contrived to edge the guest of the evening a little farther away and was rewarded in seeing Mr. Sefton execute contortions worthy of a wryneck.

"What do you play?" asked Miss Carless abruptly. She had a pleasant contralto voice, but the question was put in a somewhat perfunctory manner, as though she did not much care what answer she received.

"Apart from a little family bridge, nothing," said Pettigrew, with a serious air. "I used to attempt golf, but when my game evoked protests even from the Bar Golfing Society I thought it was time to give up."

A cheerful grin suddenly brought her masklike face to life.

"Thank God!" she said. "I've been doing nothing but talk to blasted amateurs of this and that the last half hour. Can you find me another drink?"

Once satisfied that Pettigrew had no musical pretensions whatever, Lucy Carless proved extremely good company. Her own work she took with becoming seriousness, but without conceit. She explained that she had decided to come to Markhampton overnight because she objected to traveling on the day of a concert if it could be avoided.

"Things are so rushed nowadays," she complained. "No wonder the work suffers. If it could only be managed, I should always like an extra rehearsal with the orchestra the day before."

"You couldn't possibly have had a rehearsal today," Pettigrew said. "And if it hadn't been for me you wouldn't have even got one tomorrow."

Then, stimulated by another of Ventry's potent cocktails, he launched into an account of his afternoon's exploit. His imitation of Mr. Justice Perkins was passably good to anyone who did not know the original, and Miss Carless was pleased to be amused.

"I've never been so eloquent in my life," he concluded. "It was an absolute Serjeant Buzfuz effort."

"Buzfuz?" She frowned in an effort at recollection.

"Pickwick, you know."

"Of course, yes—Pickwick. I hate Dickens."

Pettigrew was profoundly shocked.

"Hate Dickens!" he exclaimed. "Come, come! This won't do. I can understand not liking Dickens—there are quite a number of people who say they don't, though I find it hard to believe them. But one doesn't—one can't—hate him."

"I do really," Miss Carless persisted. "I had to read wads of him as a child and I simply can't stand him."

Pettigrew remembered that after all she was of foreign birth, and tried to find excuses for her.

"Perhaps you read him in translation," he said. "I can quite believe—"

"Oh no. My mother was English, you know. I was brought up to be quite bilingual."

"Then it's time you gave him one more trial. Obviously you had him forced down your throat when you were too young. I can't bear to think of your remaining in such utter darkness. Take my advice and make a fresh start on *David Copperfield*, and if you don't—"

"But that's the worst of the lot," she interrupted. "All that silly business about Dora and Agnes! Just because Dickens had got it into his head that he'd married the wrong one of two sisters. And what a fuss he made about it! Nowadays, he'd have simply got a divorce and married the other one. The Victorians were so silly about that sort of thing."

"As a matter of fact—" Pettigrew began. But at this moment the conversation, which had already lasted very much longer than any cocktail party conversation was entitled to do, was interrupted.

"My *dear* Miss Carless!" Mrs. Basset planted herself firmly between them and took control of the situation. "This is delightful! We are all so looking forward to the Mendelssohn tomorrow. Good evening, Mr. Pettigrew. And Mrs. Pettigrew"—for Eleanor, Mr. Sefton and half a dozen others had been drawn into the circle which Mrs. Basset always contrived to form around her whenever she appeared—"how well you are looking, dear! I had quite forgotten what a charming color that dress was! It suits you so well!"

Before Eleanor had had time to recover from this body blow Mrs. Basset had swept on, carrying with her Miss Carless and the rest of her attendants. Pettigrew looked up and caught Ventry's eye. He was chuckling cheerfully.

"Have another drink, old boy," he said. "And give one to your missus. She looks as though she needs it. Wonderful creatures, women, aren't they? By the way," he went on, emptying his glass and putting it down on the organ console, "you seemed to make quite a hit with Lucy. How did you manage it?"

"We were talking about Dickens," said Pettigrew rather stiffly. Ventry's brand of conversation was not one that appealed to him. He looked round to Eleanor for a means of escape, but she had been buttonholed by Mrs. Roberts, and for the moment he could see no excuse to leave him.

"Dickens? Well, that's a gambit that's never occurred to me, and I've tried a good few in my time. Still, if you have any Great Expectations in that direction, you want to look out for her husband. He's the green-eyed monster, if ever there was one." He peered through the haze of cigarette smoke at his guests. "Which reminds me, the Dixons haven't turned up yet. That ought to be quite an amusing encounter."

"Oh, you've asked them, have you?" Much though he longed to get away, Pettigrew found himself oddly fascinated by this gross creature. He began to wonder if he had not underestimated him. Perhaps he was not such a simple bundle of appetites as he

30

seemed. There was a malevolent gleam in his large blue eyes that hinted at something more than appeared on the surface.

"Asked them?" Ventry was saying. "Yes. Why not? They're all sensible people—at least, I know that two of them are. As for Nicola—well, she ought to be pleased enough with life. I suppose you saw in the paper that it was a girl?"

"That what was a girl?" asked Pettigrew in complete bewilderment.

"The widow's child—born a couple of weeks ago. Surely Mrs. Basset must have told you. She's been talking about nothing else since. Dixon's booked for a peerage now. What a game, what a game!"

The next moment he was effusively greeting a golden-haired creature who proved to be the wife of the clarinet-playing young Clarkson, and Pettigrew drifted away.

It so happened that a little later Pettigrew was present at the meeting of the past and present Mrs. Dixons and their respective husbands, which took place under the watchful and disapproving eyes of Mrs. Basset. All four, he thought, behaved very well. Dixon and Lucy, in particular, acted with admirable *sang-froid*. There was a faint flush on Nicola's cheeks as she said, "Nice to see you again, Lucy," but Lucy's "How well you're looking, Nicola!" was perfectly spoken. The auburn hair and the dark were close together for a moment and then the encounter was over. As they moved apart Pettigrew caught a simultaneous glimpse of their profiles, and the ghost of an idea flickered to the surface of his mind, to be gone again in an instant.

It recurred to him just as he was getting into bed.

"By Jove, I wonder!" he exclaimed. "Do you think she could possibly be Agnes?"

"Who could be Agnes?" said Eleanor drowsily. "Do put the light out, darling. I want to get to sleep."

"Mrs. Dixon," answered Pettigrew, obediently switching off the bedside lamp.

"Her name's Nicola," said Eleanor, falling asleep at once. But her husband remained awake for some time longer, staring up into the darkness in which Ventry's fleshy face loomed over him, dissolving into the pale, intense features of a woman who repeated the incredible words, "I hate Dickens."

"Those cocktails must have been much too strong," was his last conscious thought.

4

The Rehearsal

Pettigrew had, of course, taken a ticket for the concert; but it was not until the morning of the event that he learned that he was expected to attend the rehearsal as well. Eleanor broke the news to him at breakfast, while they were discussing the arrangements for the day.

"Mr. Dixon asked me at the party yesterday whether you could come," she remarked. "You were busy talking to someone else at the time, but I told him that you would be delighted."

"I wonder how you guessed," said Pettigrew thoughtfully.

"Honestly," Eleanor persisted, "it will be quite amusing, and I know you haven't anything else to do."

"To answer your second allegation first, I had promised myself a delightful day with the current *Law Quarterly Review*. There's an article in it entitled 'Prolegomena to Pufendorf' that simply cries out to be read."

Eleanor's brilliant blue eyes expressed the liveliest sympathy.

"Do take the *Quarterly* with you to the rehearsal then, darling," she said. "You needn't listen if you don't want to. Shall I fetch it for you? I think it's still where you put it last month to prop up the leg of your dressing table."

Pettigrew frowned. "It's high time I got the carpenter to look at that table," he observed. "It's hard enough to keep abreast with one's law without that kind of handicap. Well, I'm prepared to waive Pufendorf just for this once. But I still don't understand what use I am supposed to be at a rehearsal."

"Mr. Dixon seemed to think it would be a good plan to have you there to represent the committee, in case anything cropped up."

"I'm sure Dixon is much more capable of handling any emergency than I am. However, as you have pledged me to go, I will. Let's hope I shall be purely decorative, like a fireman at the Paris opera."

Three o'clock accordingly found the hon. treasurer once more at the City Hall. Although he had not particularly looked forward to hearing rehearsed the music which he was to listen to all over again the same evening, it proved a more interesting afternoon than he had expected. In particular, he found Clayton Evans a fascinating study. Evans at a rehearsal was something quite different from the assured, aloof figure on the rostrum with which earlier concerts had made him familiar, or from the quietly compelling expert whom he had encountered at committee meetings. This was a new Evans, at once pathetic and terrifying—pathetic in his efforts to extract from his players a standard of performance which neither they nor, probably, any musicians in the world were capable of reaching, and terrifying in the intensity that he brought to the task. He was a man strung to a pitch of excitement that was not long in communicating itself to the orchestra, and Pettigrew began to wonder before long whether the result would be a superlatively good performance or the complete collapse of all concerned from sheer nervous exhaustion.

Evans opened the proceedings with a few pointed words to the professionals.

"We begin the concert with the National Anthem, played by the whole band," he said in a taut, strained voice. "I repeat, the whole band. I am quite aware that the first number in the program is not scored for all the instruments required for the violin concerto that follows it. That makes no difference. My orchestra understands that I do not allow players to trample in and out between performances according to whether or not there is a part for them in the particular piece being played. Those of you who are not concerned in the Handel can sit and listen to it. It will be a new experience for some of you to listen to music, in any case. Is that understood?" He tapped his desk sharply. "The National Anthem, please."

"Ought one," Pettigrew asked himself, "to stand up while the National Anthem is being rehearsed?" It was the kind of delicate point on which there was no reliable authority. He glanced round and from the corner of his eye saw Lucy Carless still in her seat a row behind. As a foreigner, she was not perhaps a reliable guide. Her husband was certainly standing up, but scarcely in the manner prescribed to loyal citizens. He had his back to the platform and appeared to be conducting a *sotto voce* argument with a figure whom Pettigrew could not distinguish in the shadows. Dixon had disappeared. Pettigrew decided that it would be a work of supererogation to stand. He was glad of the decision when he realized that Evans in his then mood would tolerate nothing perfunctory in the playing of even this hackneyed tune. It took nearly ten minutes and some very bitter language before the society could be induced to perform it to his satisfaction.

"Well! I'm for it now!" said a voice in Pettigrew's ear. The figure in the shadows had materialized, and proved to be Ventry. "Have I a hangover! My fingers are going to be all thumbs this afternoon. Evans'll bite my head off: It'll be all right on the night, but what's the good of telling him that in his present state?"

"You should practice more, Mr. Ventry, and drink less!" said Lucy Carless's clear voice from the next row. "Now run along, Mr. Evans is waiting for your A."

With a grimace and a wave of his hand Ventry trotted off to the stairs leading to the organ loft, where he appeared in a time that did credit to his physical condition, hangover or no hangover. As the tuning note sounded from the organ, echoed by the instruments on the platform, Pettigrew caught snatches of what appeared to be a rather ill-tempered little conversation behind him.

"That's an odious creature," said Sefton's voice. "And so damned conceited, like all these amateurs. I've just been telling him—"

"He is not odious at all, Lawrence. I find him quite amiable."

"You find everybody amiable—that's your trouble."

"And your trouble is your absurd jealousy. As if anybody else could not see that Mr. Ventry is *épris* of Nicola. Really I feel sorry for poor Robert."

"Oh, so you feel like consoling *him*, do you?"

"Lawrence, if you say a word more you will make me nervous."

This was evidently a threat that could not be disregarded, for Sefton subsided at once. A moment later the organ concerto began.

The quick exchange of words had started a train of thought in Pettigrew's mind that distracted his attention from Handel's forthright music. Whether or not Miss Carless found Ventry too "amiable" was a matter of very little importance. It was obvious that Sefton was of an almost pathologically jealous type. But her easy assumption that Ventry had designs on Mrs. Dixon interested and surprised him not a little. He cast his mind back to the party of the day before and tried to recollect whether he had noticed anything that could support the theory. "Perhaps I am very unobservant in these matters," he thought. "Men always are, I suppose. At any rate, the husband is always said to be the last person to notice." It occurred to him that, so far as he could judge, Dixon was not likely to be an unobservant man. In that case, he gloomily reflected, the affairs of the committee were going to be unpleasantly complicated.

His meditations were interrupted by the sudden silence which marked the end of the performance. At the same time he became aware that Dixon had dropped into the seat beside him.

"Well," Dixon was saying, "I thought that went very nicely, didn't you?"

"Yes," Pettigrew replied a little guiltily. "Very well indeed."

"Ventry bungled his entry in the second movement, of course, but apart from that—" He turned to speak over his shoulder to Lucy Carless, who was preparing to go up to the platform. "You needn't hurry," he said. "Evans is bound to want that bit over again."

He was right. After a few sharp words, inaudible to the listeners, the piece was recommenced in mid-career and played through again to the end. With his mind still running on the same subject—and it was surprising, as he afterwards reflected, how much impression Miss Carless's assertion had made upon him—Pettigrew studied his neighbor with interest. Dixon seemed to be paler than usual, and there was a strained expression about the mouth that he had not noticed before. "Not that I seem to have noticed much, so far," Pettigrew told himself. It was probably imagination, and in any case no affair of his. None the less, in the pause that succeeded the repetition of the Handel concerto, and while Lucy Carless was making her way to the platform, he found himself saying, almost involuntarily, "Your wife isn't here this afternoon?"

It was an idiotic question to ask, as Pettigrew realized at once. There was no earthly reason why Mrs. Dixon should attend the rehearsal. She did not play, nor was she on the committee. But Dixon did not appear to find it strange.

"No," he said. "She isn't. She's coming to the concert this evening, of course. I've left her the car. I shan't be going home before the concert myself. I shall hang around and see that the pros are being properly looked after."

"I see." Pettigrew tried not to look as bored as he felt. He had hardly expected such a flood of supremely uninteresting information on his personal affairs from a man normally so reserved as Dixon. It seemed so out of character as to make him feel almost uneasy. Why should the fellow expect him to be interested in whether he went home before the concert or not? It sounded almost as if—

"I say," said Ventry's thick voice from just behind, "that was a rotten bloomer I made in the second movement, wasn't it? I can't think how I came to do it. Thought I knew the old Alleluia backwards. But it sounded all right the second time though, didn't it?"

Pettigrew was just beginning to assure him that it had sounded perfect when Sefton's voice broke in.

"Will you please be quiet?" he said in an icy tone. "My wife is about to play."

As though to add point to his words, he rose from his seat and moved to the far end of the row.

"Disagreeable blighter," remarked Ventry reflectively. "'My wife is about to play,' indeed! She's much too good for him—if *you* don't mind my saying so, old man."

The last remark was addressed to Dixon, and Pettigrew wondered whether he had ever heard anything in quite such bad taste. Dixon said nothing in reply. He did not even turn his head, continuing to stare straight in front of him towards the platform where Lucy Carless was finishing tuning her violin, but a red spot on his cheeks showed that the allusion had not been lost on him. The awkward silence was broken a few seconds later by the sharp tap of Evans's baton.

"We're off!" murmured the unabashed Ventry. "Quiet, boys!"

For the next thirty minutes Pettigrew forgot his concern over Dixon's matrimonial affairs, his annoyance with Ventry and his own resentment at being made to attend the rehearsal against his will. He knew nothing whatever of the technique of the violin, but Lucy Carless had not played half a dozen bars before he realized that he was listening to a superb executant playing at the very top of her form. The warm romantic appeal of Mendelssohn suited her. The orchestra, taking fire from her, played with a brilliance that it is not often given to amateurs to achieve. Pettigrew had recently more than once heard the concerto described by the austerer members of the society as "popular music," and being himself something of an intellectual snob, had joined in the superior sniffs that naturally accompanied the words. Recollecting it now, he told himself that it was only right and proper that such music should be popular, and hoped he would have the courage to say so when he next heard the phrase.

The performance ended in a pleasant scene of mutual congratulations between soloist, orchestra and conductor—all the more pleasant because there was no audience to make them seem artificial and theatrical. Lucy seemed genuinely pleased with herself and her fellow players. The orchestra—at least the amateur portion of it—appeared quite astonished at its own performance. Even Evans looked almost satisfied. He had taken the concerto straight through without more than a minimum pause between the movements and had so far refrained from comment or criticism. Now, mopping his brow with his handkerchief, he endeavored to say something above the hubbub of conversation that had broken out. "Cellos, you *must* remember, in the slow movement—" he began, but broke off, with a reluctant smile. "But you were jolly good, all of you!" he exclaimed. Mrs. Basset, who was usually a figure of grim concentration on the platform, so far forgot herself as to wave her bow gaily in his direction. "We'll remember, won't we, girls?" she cried archly—an exclamation that produced a shout of surprised laughter from her fellows, who would as soon have expected to be called "girls" by the jubilee statue of Queen Victoria in the Market Square.

Looking at all the flushed and happy faces, seeing Eleanor, in her humble seat among the second violins, with her features transfigured by pure pleasure, Pettigrew realized for the first time what it was that made all the trouble and drudgery of practice and rehearsal worth while for these people. He envied them deeply. "They hardly need a concert with an audience," he thought. "Making the music is the fun for them." He suddenly felt an outsider, and alone.

At that moment he realized that he was, in fact, alone. Dixon,

Ventry and Sefton had each made his way to the platform. Although the rehearsal was not over—there was still the Mozart symphony to come—by common consent there was a pause at this point. Some relaxation was obviously necessary after the tension of the performance, such as would be provided at the concert itself by the interval. The players left their seats, stretched their legs, lit cigarettes and chatted to one another or joined in the informal reception which Lucy Carless, who seemed refreshed rather than exhausted by her efforts, was now holding on the platform. Pettigrew was amused to see that Sefton had established himself firmly by her elbow, and that this had not prevented Ventry from approaching her and engaging her in a short but animated conversation. Dixon was somewhere near, but soon lost to sight in the throng.

Pettigrew decided to go up on to the platform himself, not to inflict himself upon the heroine of the moment, but with the more sober purpose of keeping his wife company. He found Eleanor talking to Mrs. Roberts. They were on the first tier of raised seats immediately behind the stage and Pettigrew joined them there. Standing beside them he was within a few yards of Lucy and Evans, and consequently had an excellent view of the unpleasant scene that followed a few minutes later.

It began, as he had reason to recollect later, with Mrs. Roberts, though it would be obviously unfair to consider that excellent lady as anything but an innocent agent in the affair. He had only exchanged a few words with her when they were joined by a small, dark man who had stepped down from the ranks of the wind instruments above and behind them.

"Well, Mrs. Roberts," said the new arrival in a heavily accented voice, "did you find it good?"

"It was splendid, really *splendid*," said Mrs. Roberts. "How superbly she plays! If only we are as good this evening—Mr. Pettigrew, I don't believe you have met Mr. Zbar—Zbar—I'm sorry, but I'm so silly about names."

"Zbartorowski. I am pleased to meet you, sir."

Pettigrew remembered the name, though he could not have guaranteed to pronounce it. This melancholy-looking fellow was the protégé of Mrs. Roberts who had been the subject of discussion at the committee meeting. He shook his hand and wondered what was the proper conversational gambit for an unmusical English lawyer when introduced to a Polish clarinetist. Mrs. Roberts, however, saved him the trouble of talking.

"You must feel very proud of her," she said.

"Please?"

"Proud of Miss Carless. She is Polish, isn't she? At least, I understood—"

"Yes, yes, that is true," said Zbartorowski, looking more melancholy than ever. "At least, partly so."

"Do you know her?" Mrs. Roberts went on.

"No, I do not precisely know her. I—"

"Oh, then you must let me introduce you to her. I am sure she would be so interested to meet a fellow countryman."

"Indeed not, Mrs. Roberts. I assure you, there is no need. You will excuse me—"

It looked as though the bashful Zbartorowski was about to scramble back to his safe eyrie above, but at that moment he was hailed by Dixon from the stage.

"Ah, Zbartorowski," he called. "I was looking for you. Just come here a moment, would you?"

In spite of his insignificant appearance Dixon could be quite masterful when he chose, and the Pole obeyed him quite meekly. He stepped down onto the platform and allowed Dixon to take him by the arm. Before he knew what had happened to him he found himself being steered between the violinists' music desks right up to where Lucy Carless was taking her leave of Clayton Evans.

"Oh, Lucy," said Dixon, breaking in on her a trifle brusquely, "before you go I'd like you to meet a compatriot of yours—a veteran of the old Warsaw Opera House—Mr. Zbartorowski."

The words were hardly uttered before it was obvious that a

41

horrible blunder had been made. At the mention of the name, Lucy's hand, which she had automatically extended, dropped to her side, and her face suddenly lost its animation and became set and almost sullen.

"Zbartorowski?" she repeated, and added a question in Polish. Whatever the words meant, they brought a sudden touch of color to the cheeks of the other. He replied in the same language. His words were few and, so far as his large and interested audience could gather, not particularly polite. There could certainly be no doubt of their effect on the person to whom they were addressed. Her next sentence, delivered in a low, clear, carrying voice, could have been nothing but a deadly insult in any language. At this point Dixon interjected something in Polish, apparently in an endeavor to act as a peacemaker, but his unfortunate effort only added fuel to the flames. Zbartorowski, his face convulsed with passion, began to hurl what must have been remarkably violent and picturesque aspersions at Lucy; Lucy, obviously keeping her hands off him with difficulty, punctuated his remarks with a selection of what were evidently the most wounding epithets in the Polish vocabulary. It was a shocking, if exhilarating, display of temperament, and fortunately for those who watched and listened, it ended as suddenly as it had started.

"It is enough!" cried Lucy, turning abruptly from her tormentor to Evans. "Either this man leaves the orchestra or I do not play tonight!"

Dixon made one more effort to repair the harm he had done.

"Have a heart, Lucy," he said. "You needn't look at him, you know. And God knows where we should get another clarinet from at this time of day."

"I'll trouble you to leave my wife alone. You've done quite enough harm already!" Lawrence Sefton was white with anger.

Dixon was about to reply when Zbartorowski broke in.

"You need not concern yourselves," he answered. "I do not choose myself to perform." And with a remarkable assumption of dignity he stalked off the platform amid a sudden silence.

Then Clayton Evans spoke. "We will continue the rehearsal," he said sharply. "Kindly get back to your places, everyone. Dixon, you will have to find a clarinetist for this evening. Be as quick as you can, please. Now, ladies and gentlemen, the Mozart."

He tapped his desk with his baton.

5

In Search of a Clarinetist

"This," said Dixon gloomily, "is a pretty kettle of fish."

Pettigrew, Ventry and he, the only members of the committee who were not at that moment rehearsing Mozart's Prague Symphony, had adjourned to one of the offices opening out of the concert room to discuss the situation.

"I don't suppose I ever made such a bloomer in my life," he went on, with a crestfallen expression quite foreign to his usually self-satisfied manner. "I feel a prize idiot. But how the hell was I to know?"

"What exactly happened?" asked Pettigrew.

"I rather gathered," said Ventry with a heavy attempt at sarcasm, "that Mrs. Roberts's boy friend and Miss Carless failed to hit it off. I may be wrong, but that was how it looked to me."

Dixon disregarded him.

"What happened was this," he said to Pettigrew. "Lucy's father, old Count Ignacz, fell foul of Pilsudski, way back in the twenties. He lost his property, spent quite a bit of time in prison, and eventually, because he still wouldn't behave like a good boy, died in a highly convenient accident. Lucy always maintained he was murdered, and I dare say she was right. I knew all about that, of course. What I didn't know—and I could kick myself for not finding out—was that friend Zbartorowski had been mixed up in the affair."

"Mixed up in what way?" Pettigrew asked.

"To judge from Lucy's remarks just now, mixed up to the extent of being her father's assassin—but I don't know that that need necessarily be true. I gathered from what he said that his family were originally tenants on the Carlessoff estate, which in the Poland of that period was quite enough excuse for having a grudge against him. I rather think Zbartorowski had affiliations with the political police and took the opportunity to turn the old man in when he got the chance. But the details don't matter."

"No," said Ventry. "All that matters now is that we are short of a clarinet."

"That's the position." Dixon looked at his watch. "Good Lord! It's nearly half past four now. How the hell are we going to find one by eight?"

It would be difficult, Pettigrew felt, to find anyone in England less likely than himself to be able to answer such an appeal. Nevertheless, with a sudden effort of memory, he unexpectedly found himself able to contribute a suggestion.

"Hadn't you a friend who played the clarinet, Ventry?" he said. "I seem to remember, at the first committee meeting—"

"Yes, of course," said Ventry. "Silly of me to have forgotten. Young Clarkson is our man. I'll pop round to him now. He'll get an awful kick out of it, coming in at the last moment."

"Young Clarkson be damned!" said Dixon, with surprising ferocity. "You know as well as I do that he's quite hopeless, and the idea of his coming in at the last moment when he hasn't so much as seen the music is quite ridiculous. He'd be enough to wreck the whole show. If you've got no better ideas than that, Ventry, you might as well go home and leave us to it."

Ventry's face went an angry red, and for a moment it looked as though he were about to lose his temper. After a short silence, however, he appeared to think better of it, and when he spoke it was in quiet, indifferent tones. "Very well," he said. "If that's what you feel about it, I'll be off. I don't care all that much for Clarkson, anyway. See you this evening."

When he had gone Dixon turned to Pettigrew with a sigh of relief.

"Now perhaps we can get on with it," he said. "All the same, I don't know how we're going to get a man from London at this time of day. I had quite a job finding even one clarinetist when I was fixing this up weeks ago—that was why I jumped at the Polish blighter when I got the chance. But I've got a few names here, and their telephone numbers, and we'll just have to see what we can do."

The ensuing half hour was, for Pettigrew at least, one of increasing boredom and frustration. The Markhampton telephone system was automatic, and commendably efficient for local calls. The exchange, however, was apt to be somewhat sluggish in answering when it was a question of putting through a trunk call, and the London line seemed to be exceptionally busy. One after another, with maddening delays, they tried the numbers suggested by Dixon, but without success. From two of them there was no reply. A third was answered by a deaf half-wit, who eventually disclosed that the number was that of a Bloomsbury boarding-house, where the musician in question had never been heard of. A fourth line proved to be out of order. And so it went on. Finally Dixon confessed himself beaten.

"I give it up," he said. "Either my list is hopelessly out of date, or all the clarinetists in London are out of town."

"It looks as though we'll be driven back on Clarkson after all," remarked Pettigrew.

"The hell we will!" retorted Dixon, stung to renewed energy by the suggestion. "We're not beaten yet. I've just remembered, there's a fellow over at Whitsea who would do the trick, if we can get hold of him."

"It's quite a distance from here to Whitsea," said Pettigrew.

46

"I've done the journey often enough on circuit. If we can find him, do you think he could get here in time for the concert?"

"I think so, yes. We could send a car to fetch him at Eastbury Junction. That's on the main line, isn't it?" Dixon was hunting through his dog-eared notebook. "Look here, can you do me a kindness? Get through to this chap on the telephone while I rake up a railway timetable. Here's his number—Whitsea 0497. The name's Jenkinson. Time's getting on, and—"

The door closed behind him. Pettigrew, left alone in the office, looked at the telephone on the table with acute distaste. He felt that he had been pitchforked into a business which he did not in the least understand and about which he really cared nothing, merely through yielding to a fatal impulse of good nature. Why had he ever allowed himself to be connected with the confounded Orchestral Society? Why had he consented to come to the rehearsal, instead of staying quietly at home, reading the Prolegomena to Pufendorf? He was feeling distinctly allergic to clarinets, and didn't care two hoots whether Mendelssohn's violin concerto was played with one of them or two, or none. What was more, he was morally certain that nobody in the audience would notice the difference. Since, however, in this ridiculous world the matter did seem to have some importance, he supposed he might as well do what was expected of him. Resignedly he picked up the receiver and dialed the code number for a trunk call.

From his recent experience he had every reason to hope that the connection would be delayed long enough to enable Dixon to return and do his own dirty work, but he was disappointed. On this occasion the telephone service chose to function with unaccustomed speed, and within less than a minute a thin, precise voice was saying in Pettigrew's ear, "This is Whitsea, 0497."

"Can I speak to Mr. Jenkinson?"

"This is Jenkinson speaking. Who are you?"

"My name is Pettigrew, but you won't know me."

"No." The voice was quite clear on that point. "I don't know you."

47

"Well, I'm speaking for Mr. Dixon, of Markhampton. I think you know him, all right."

"I'm fairly positive I don't know anyone called Dixon. What is his Christian name?"

"Robert."

"Then I certainly don't know him."

Pettigrew felt inclined to giggle.

"We don't seem to be getting on very well, do we?" he said weakly.

"No, we don't. Have you got the wrong number, by any chance?"

"I don't think so. You *are* Mr. Jenkinson, aren't you?"

"I have said so already."

"Do you play the thingummy?"

"The what?"

"I beg your pardon, the clarinet, I mean."

"I do. And a number of other instruments besides, but not the one you mentioned first."

"Never mind about that. The point is, we want a clarinet badly."

"I have not one to spare, and if I had, I wouldn't sell it."

"I'm afraid I expressed myself badly. I mean, we want someone to play the clarinet."

"I see. And who are 'we'?"

"I'm so sorry, I ought to have mentioned that in the first place. The Markshire Orchestral Society."

"Now that," said the voice, with a distinct air of triumph, "I have heard of. Clayton Evans, is it not?"

"That's right," said Pettigrew, like an exhausted swimmer whose foot at last touches bottom. "Clayton Evans it is."

"Why didn't you mention him before? Of course I shall be only too glad to play for Evans at any time he wants me. Just let Potter and Fullbright know."

"Potter and who?" With a sickening feeling Pettigrew realized that he was out of his depth again.

"Potter and Fullbright," the voice repeated, with the air of one patiently addressing a very stupid child. "My agents. *The* agents. You must have heard of Potter and Fullbright, surely."

"No, I don't know Potter and Fullbright." (I'm getting the hang of this game, thought Pettigrew. The score must be about thirty-all now.) The voice went on: "Well, they're in the book. Just ring them up whenever you want me, and I'll come, if I'm free. Is that understood?"

"No!" cried Pettigrew violently, just in time to prevent Jenkinson ringing off. From the corner of his eye he could see Dixon come in, flourishing a railway guide. "Just hold on a minute." He thrust the instrument at Dixon. "For Heaven's sake deal with this," he said. "It's beyond me."

Feeling like a very junior clerk when the senior partner takes charge, he thankfully relinquished the conduct of affairs to the expert.

"This is Dixon here."

"I don't know—" With unholy pleasure Pettigrew heard the faint voice taking up its cue once more.

"No, of course, you don't. I got your name from Potter and Fullbright."

"The other man who was talking to me—Peter somebody or other—had never *heard* of Potter and Fullbright," said the voice querulously.

"Oh, *him*," said Dixon, brutally. The junior clerk felt more junior than ever. "Never mind about him. I am speaking for Clayton Evans from Markhampton. He's in a spot of bother. His first clarinet has walked out on him, and he must have one tonight. Can you come over straightaway? It's all routine stuff—Mendelssohn violin concerto, a spot of Handel, Mozart—nothing troublesome....What?...Yes, yes, of course, union fees and all expenses. You can? Good. Now, look. There's a six thirty-five train from Whitsea, due in at Eastbury Junction at seven twenty-nine. It's not more than twenty minutes' run from there to Markhampton and I'll have a car to meet you. That'll just give you time. Splendid. Many thanks. Good-by."

Dixon put down the receiver and wiped his forehead with his handkerchief.

"That's settled, thank goodness!" he said. "I say, Pettigrew, I'm very much obliged to you for helping me out."

"Don't mention it," said Pettigrew, weakly.

"Now the only thing that's left is to find a car to meet the train. That may be rather a job on a night like this. Everyone will be hiring cars to get to the concert."

"Shall I ring up Farren's?" asked Pettigrew, naming the largest firm of car-renters in the city.

"Don't bother. I'll do it. Do you know their number, by any chance?"

"I've got it written down, as it happens," said Pettigrew. "It's 2203."

"Thanks." Dixon picked up the receiver once more, but as he did so there was an interruption. For the last few minutes Pettigrew had been aware of the fact that the office in which they were speaking had become noticeably quieter. This was due, he now realized, to the cessation of the half-heard strains of music which had formed the background to their conversation. Evidently the rehearsal had come to an end. Now Evans, with Mrs. Basset in dutiful attendance, came into the room. Evans looked tired, but quite calm and cheerful.

"You still here, Dixon?" he said. "Look here, I don't think you need worry about that clarinet."

"Not worry!" Dixon's face was a study.

"No. I've worked it out in my mind. We can promote the second clarinet to first, of course, so that only leaves the second's part to consider. Well, in the Mendelssohn there are only two or three passages of importance, and I can arrange with the second oboe to cover them. I don't suppose anyone in the audience will notice the difference. The Handel doesn't matter a damn—there aren't any clarinets in the original scoring, anyway—and the Mozart—"

50

"My good Evans," said Dixon, in tones that made Mrs. Basset blench. "You told me to get another clarinet. Pettigrew and I have been trying for the last forty minutes to find one. Now we have at last succeeded, you tell me not to worry. That is a bit too much!"

"Oh, you have found one? Good," replied Evans, quite unperturbed. "Who is he, by the way?"

"Jenkinson, of the Whitsea Philharmonic. I'm just about ringing up for a car to meet him at Eastbury. What did you say Farren's number was, Pettigrew?"

"2203."

"2203," repeated Dixon as he spun the dial. "Hullo, hullo! Is that Farren's? Have you a car free this evening to meet the seven twenty-nine at Eastbury?...Good. You're to meet a gentleman called Jenkinson and bring him to the City Hall, stage entrance. You'll attend to that? Oh, and send the bill to Mr. Pettigrew....Thank you. Good-by."

Dixon rang off with an air of triumph.

"Well," observed Evans, "that saves me monkeying about with the oboe parts, anyway. Thank you, Dixon. I'm going home to change now. By the way," he paused in the door, "I'm afraid Miss Carless was rather upset over that affair at rehearsal. You won't be seeing her again before the performance, I suppose?"

"I?" said Dixon quickly. "No, of course not. Why should I?"

"I just thought I'd mention it—I think she wants time to cool off. Because she particularly asked that she should be left entirely alone in the artist's room until her time comes to go on to the platform. So if you are around then, keep out. I've warned all the orchestra."

Dixon grinned.

"You needn't worry about me," he said. "That's an old custom of Lucy's, and nothing whatever to do with my *faux pas* over Zbartorowski. She always immures herself before she plays. It's a form of nerves, I suppose. Not even husbands admitted—let alone has-beens."

"I see," said Evans. He remained standing irresolutely in the

51

doorway for a moment, a reflective frown creasing his forehead.

"Is there anything else?" asked Dixon with a yawn. "Because if not—"

"I don't think so," Evans said slowly. "At least—there was something bothering me—a question of tempo, I think—but I can't remember now what it was." He came out of his abstraction abruptly. "Mrs. Basset, I think you were kind enough to say you would give me a lift home."

He left, and Pettigrew, who felt as though he had been shut up in the little office for half a lifetime, made haste to follow his example.

6

A Concert Interrupted

It was with a feeling of anticlimax that Pettigrew returned to the City Hall at about a quarter to eight that evening. After the troubles that the rehearsal had produced he felt that the performance, however successful, would be comparatively flat. If he had not already paid for his ticket, he told himself, he would have been much inclined to stay away. He knew too much, however, to confide his sentiments to Eleanor, who was pardonably excited at the prospect of taking part in her first concert.

He left his wife at the artists' entrance, and saw her carried away in a flood of eager, elated amateurs, leavened by a few businesslike, phlegmatic professionals, before going round to the main door. The hall, he found, was already filling rapidly, and from his seat in the gallery he looked down on a sea of heads. Like everyone else who has been admitted, for however brief a space, behind the scenes at any spectacle, he wondered how many of the chattering, expectant throng had any idea of the amount of trouble and confusion that had had to be gone through to produce the two hours of entertainment which they were about to enjoy. "It'll be all right on the night," he told himself cheerfully, and settled down to read, with more admiration than understanding, the severely technical analytical notes which Clayton Evans had contributed to the program.

His reading was shortly interrupted by someone pushing past him to the vacant seat at his side. Looking up, he saw, not without pleasure, that it was Nicola Dixon. She was, he told himself, the ideal neighbor for such a function—someone who would neither talk too much nor expect to be talked to, and who was at the same time agreeable to look at. Extremely agreeable to look at, he reflected, as he turned to greet her. Indeed, though he had always been sensible of the fact that she was a very handsome young woman, he did not think he had ever seen her to so much advantage before. Even to such a thoroughly unobservant man as himself it was apparent that she was exceptionally well turned out for the occasion. But it was not only that her dress—which Pettigrew could not have begun to describe—made the rather dowdy Markhampton matrons in the hall seem positively shabby in comparison, nor that she had obviously taken considerable pains with her make-up. In some indefinable way her whole countenance had gained in attractiveness. Her eyes were brighter, the color of her cheeks more vivid and her usual rather languid charm had given place to an expression of animation and awareness that was enormously—Pettigrew searched for the word in his mind and was mildly shocked with himself when he found it—enormously seductive. It seemed strange that the prospect of a mere concert in the City Hall could so enliven her, he thought; her enthusiasm for music must be greater than he had supposed—greater, certainly, than her husband's.

Reminded of Robert Dixon's existence, Pettigrew remarked, "Your husband isn't with you?"

Nicola shook her sleek auburn head.

"He never sits with me at these shows," she explained. "He has a seat downstairs, somewhere near the back, so that he can scurry round to see that things are in order. Talking of scurrying, I thought I shouldn't make it myself tonight. The damned car park was so crowded, I had a job to find a place." She looked impatiently at her wrist watch as if, now that she had arrived, she grudged every moment before the concert should begin.

Meanwhile, things had been happening on the stage below. The members of the orchestra had assembled on the platform and the air was filled with fragmentary toots and twiddles as they tried over passages on their instruments. The exciting little turmoil of sound subsided, and was followed by a splutter of applause for Miss Porteous, who made her way to the leader's desk at the head of the violins, striving to appear at ease, but pink with suppressed emotion. An expectant hush settled on the hall, and then there was a storm of clapping as Clayton Evans was seen at the back of the stage, which continued, growing in intensity, until he reached the rostrum. He acknowledged the greeting with the briefest of bows, turned, tapped his desk, and, almost before the applause had died away, brought orchestra and audience to their feet with the drum-roll that preluded the National Anthem.

It occurred to Pettigrew at this point to wonder for the first time since he had entered the hall whether the elusive clarinetist had put in an appearance. Jenkinson had certainly sounded a very positive and reliable individual on the telephone, not the kind of man who—once the little matter of Potter and Fullbright had been cleared up—would be likely to fail to keep an appointment. Still, he wished to be sure, and he scanned the ranks of the players with an anxious eye. Unfortunately, the gallery was almost at a level with the line of large chandeliers which illuminated the main body of the hall, and this made his view of the back rows of the orchestra rather difficult. None the less, as he looked along them it did seem as though, in the right-hand corner, next to the flutes, there was a blank space. He looked again, tried to account for all the players who obviously were there, in order to establish whether one was not. Two flutes—that was easy. Two of those fellows who blow into a little tube and make a kind of grunting sound—bassoons, of course, that was the name. And lastly, twisting his neck to dodge the blinding chandelier, he could distinguish three men blowing straight downwards into their instruments, and not sideways like flutes, or at an angle, like bassoons. Oboes and clarinets—and which was which and what was the difference between them he never could remember, though Eleanor had explained often enough. Three? Surely there should be four—two of each—unless for some obscure reason the oboe was a solitary, and didn't go about in pairs like all his fellows? No, that would not do. Evans had distinctly said two oboes. It could only mean that the orchestra was short of a clarinet after all.

He had just reached this melancholy conclusion, and the last bars of the National Anthem were crashing out, when there was a slight stir in the right-hand back row of the orchestra. A desk was pushed on one side, two brass instruments and their players edged apart to make a gangway, and as the orchestra sat down, Pettigrew realized that the three players had become four. Jenkinson had cut it fine, but he had succeeded. It was most satisfactory. From where he sat Pettigrew could not distinguish his face, beyond the fact that it was ornamented with horn-rimmed spectacles, but he promised himself the pleasure of meeting him after the concert. From their brief chat on the telephone, he judged him to be quite a character. Meanwhile, he could sit back and enjoy the music and forget that he was a committee-man. Everything from now on was going according to plan.

It took less than half a minute for Pettigrew, in common with the rest of the audience, to realize that everything was not, after all, going according to plan. In his anxiety over that comparatively minor orchestra figure, the first clarinetist, he had taken for granted the presence of everybody else essential to the performance. It was Nicola Dixon who drew his attention to the fact that someone else was absent.

"Good Lord!" she exclaimed in an anxious voice. "Where on earth's Billy Ventry?"

Looking towards the organ loft, Pettigrew saw to his horror that it was unoccupied.

To be even a spectator at a public function when a serious hitch occurs produces in the normal mind a certain feeling of distress, and Pettigrew, who rated himself as something more than a mere spectator, felt acutely uncomfortable. What added to his discomfort was the fact that one of the last people in the hall to realize that something had gone radically wrong was Clayton Evans himself. With serene confidence he stood there, Handel's score open before him. He threw back his head in a characteristic gesture, gave his usual sharp tap to his desk to bring his orchestra to attention, extended his hands and looked hopefully in the direction of the organ loft.

"This is awful!" muttered Pettigrew. "The poor devil's as blind as a bat. Won't anyone tell him?"

Miss Porteous in fact told him, just as it seemed that the Alleluia Organ Concerto would be embarked upon without an organist. There was a hasty colloquy between the two, while a buzz of conversation broke out in the audience. Evans produced a watch from his pocket, held it close to his nose, replaced it, laid the baton down on his desk and stood for a few moments irresolute. His back was to the audience, but even from the gallery it could be seen that his long, sensitive hands were shaking.

"He's not going to wait for him, surely," Mrs. Dixon murmured. "I've never known Evans—"

Evans was not going to wait. With a visible effort he straightened his bent back and turned to face the audience.

"Ladies and gentlemen," he said, his voice well under control, "I am afraid it has become necessary to alter the order of the program. We shall begin with the Prague Symphony of Mozart. The Handel Organ Concerto will be played after the interval."

There was the usual polite applause that greets announcements of this nature, a hasty shifting of scores on the music desks of the players. Then Evans swung round to face his orchestra once more and the first concert of the season presented by the Markshire Symphony Orchestra was at last begun.

Those better able to judge than Pettigrew considered the performance of the Prague Symphony a highly creditable one. The last-minute alteration in the arrangements had not been without its effect on the nerves of some of the amateurs, and there was some ragged playing at the outset. But before the first movement had run half its course Evans had asserted his authority, the orchestra was well in hand, and the music was being rendered with all the crispness and delicacy that Mozart demands. The applause at the end of the performance was a good deal more than polite.

None the less, to nine tenths of the audience the symphony had been no more than an hors d'oeuvre, and a rather prolonged hors d'oeuvre at that. They had paid their money primarily to hear Mendelssohn's Violin Concerto—or rather, they had paid to hear Lucy Carless playing Mendelssohn, and the rearrangement, by inserting a substantial symphony before it, instead of a brief curtain raiser, had left them restless and dissatisfied.

Clayton Evans must have felt the impatience of the audience, for his acknowledgment of their applause at the conclusion of the symphony was noticeably brief. He favored them with a curt bow, laid down his baton and before the clapping had died away strode off the platform. It was his invariable practice to introduce visiting soloists to their audience. Like all good conductors he had something of the showman in his make-up, and he had brought to a fine art the technique of escorting a distinguished visitor on to the platform. The air of deftly compounded patronage and deference with which he performed the task was the result of long practice. The less reverent members of his orchestra imitated it among themselves when they foregathered for rehearsals. His faithful public regarded it as one of the high lights of the evening. As Evans disappeared behind the players in the direction of the artist's room, they sat back contented and expectant in their seats. "This," their expressions seemed to say, "is what we were waiting for!"

They had to wait a good deal longer than usual.

After a delay that seemed interminable, but could not in fact have lasted more than a minute or two, a burst of applause greeted the conductor's reappearance. It ceased abruptly as quickly as it had begun. Evans was alone. He came slowly on to the platform, his shoulders bowed, his chin upon his chest, walking like a man in a dream. There was dead silence in the hall as he dragged himself on to the rostrum. His hands gripping the rail as though he would have fallen without support, he stood there for a moment speechless—a silent man facing a silent gathering. Then he spoke, in a hoarse voice that was barely recognizable. His words were muttered, but in the utter stillness of the hall they were audible enough.

"There has been an accident," he was heard to say. "A terrible accident. I want a doctor immediately."

7

Introducing Trimble

A gale of rationalization, blowing strongly from Whitehall a few years previously, had swept away, with many other things, the Markhampton City Police Force. It was consequently a detective-inspector of the City Division of the Markshire County Constabulary who came in answer to the urgent message, which reached him just as he was about to leave his headquarters after his day's duty. Inspector Trimble was a young man for his rank in a service in which promotion is normally slow. He was also energetic and ambitious. His predecessor in the City force had been none of these things, and had gratefully accepted the offer of an early retirement on pension extended to him when the County Police took over. That easygoing man had not gone altogether unregretted by his subordinates, who viewed the bustling "new bloke" with a certain suspicion. Trimble was well aware that he had yet to prove himself in their eyes, and he was on the whole pleased that on this occasion he should be accompanied by an elderly, skeptical sergeant of the old dispensation. He had been seeking an opportunity to impress Sergeant Tate with the virtues of the County organization in general, and of its detective-inspector in particular, and perhaps this case would provide it.

The inspector drove to the artists' entrance of the City Hall. A white-faced porter opened the door to him. Inside, he found himself in a corridor packed to overflowing with men and women who fell abruptly silent as he entered. Their anxious faces turned to follow his progress as he pushed his way through.

There were doors opening out of the corridor on either side. Outside one of these, to his right as he entered, and in the direction of the concert hall, stood a police constable, red-faced and important, who drew himself up and saluted as Trimble approached.

"She's in here, sir," he said. "Dr. Cutbush is with the body. Nothing has been touched. I've—"

Trimble cut him short with a curt nod.

"I'll take your report later," he said. "Stay where you are until I send for you."

Behind his back, Sergeant Tate favored the constable with a sardonic grin as Trimble passed through the door, a slim, assured figure—possibly a shade too assured, ill-wishers might have thought.

The artist's room was a small, square apartment. Its paneled walls were unbroken by windows, a skylight in the lofty ceiling taking their place. There was a second door opposite the one by which the inspector had entered. The furniture consisted of a table, two or three plain chairs and a deep armchair. On the table were several vases of flowers and a violin in its open case. Dr. Cutbush was sitting on one of the hard chairs. In the armchair was the huddled form of Lucy Carless.

Trimble looked quickly round the room before he approached the body. Then he walked across to the opposite door and opened it. He found himself looking into another corridor, roughly parallel to the one he had just left, but curving at either end to conform to the shape of the stage behind which it ran. After establishing the lay of the land he closed the door again and locked it from the inside.

"Has anybody been through this door since the body was found?" he asked.

"Well, I have, naturally, since I came from the body of the hall," replied the doctor in a gentle, deprecating voice. "But so far as I am aware, no one else."

"I see. Well, doctor, what have you to tell me?"

"Very little, I am afraid, further than that life was extinct when I arrived. The cause of death, as you can see"—here, he rose, walked to the armchair, and with wonderful tenderness pulled aside the mass of dark hair which shrouded the terribly distorted face—"the cause of death was evidently strangulation. What appears to be a silk stocking has been very tightly tied around the neck. But I have touched nothing. Your own medical officer will deal with that in due course, no doubt." He let the hair fall back into place. "A sad loss, Inspector," he said with a sigh. "She was a great artist."

"How long would you say had elapsed between death and when you found her?"

Dr. Cutbush shook his head.

"I am afraid forensic medicine has never been a subject of mine," he said. "It was certainly not long—half an hour perhaps, but little more than that. There again, I must leave you to the specialist."

"I see. Well, Doctor, if you will give your name and address to Sergeant Tate here he will take a formal statement from you in due course. I needn't keep you any longer now."

"Thank you. And may I take my little girl with me?"

"Your little girl?" asked Trimble.

"She is one of the orchestra—a first violin. I am sure she will have been terribly upset, and I should like to get her away."

"The orchestra?" Trimble stroked his chin uncertainly. "Sergeant, do you know the layout of this building?"

"Yes, sir, very well. I've sung 'The Messiah' in it many a time."

"How do the orchestra get on to the platform?"

"By that corridor you were looking at just now. Either end of it leads on to the stage—right or left side, according. With steps to take you up to the back rows."

"That was what I thought. Then anyone going on to the stage might pass this door on the way?"

"That's right. And conversely, anyone coming out of this room might go on to the stage just as if he hadn't. There are two or three other doors leading into that corridor, you see."

Slightly nettled at his sergeant's emphasizing the obvious, Trimble turned to Dr. Cutbush.

"I am afraid I shall have to keep the orchestra here for the time being," he said. "But I hope it won't be for long. Meanwhile you can join your daughter, if you wish."

The doctor having departed, Trimble carried out a brief but intensive search of the room. He was conscious as he did so that the sergeant, while apparently assisting him, was at the same time subjecting him to a wordless but lively criticism. It was all the more annoying, therefore, that the search proved entirely fruitless. Nothing whatever in the room was out of order. Everything was perfectly normal—except for the still, silent figure in the armchair. Finally he sent for the constable at the door and ordered Sergeant Tate to take his place until another uniformed man from headquarters could arrive to relieve him. The constable was evidently bursting with information. He took a deep breath and began:

"I was on duty outside the main entrance, sir, when I became aware of a certain commotion inside."

"What sort of commotion?"

"There were some screams and hysterics in the audience, sir, and a St. John's Ambulance man reported that a lady had fainted. I went into the hall, and ascertained that a doctor had been sent for to the artist's room. I accordingly made my way round to the back and came in through the stage door. I found Dr. Cutbush here with Mr. Evans, the conductor. Also Mr. Sefton."

"Mr. Sefton?"

"I gathered that he was the husband of the deceased, sir. He was in a somewhat excited condition. I had some difficulty in persuading him to leave the room. He was making a number of wild accusations against a variety of individuals, including Mr. Evans."

"Very well. And what action did you take?"

"Having ascertained from the doctor that life was extinct, sir, and that there was adequate reason to suspect that a felony had been committed, I deemed it my duty to take charge."

"My question," said Trimble icily, "was—what action did you take?"

"I requested a member of the City Hall staff who had accompanied me from the main entrance to notify headquarters by telephone, sir—not liking to leave the scene of the occurrence unguarded. Meanwhile, while awaiting assistance, I suggested to Mr. Evans that he should announce that the concert was abandoned and cause the audience to disperse, which I understand they have done, to a large extent."

"Yes?"

"I then posted myself outside the door in the position in which you found me, sir, in order to prevent any interference. The matter was a little complicated by reason of the fact that the members of the orchestra had by this time come off the platform and were milling around, if I may so put it, sir, many of them carrying musical instruments of various shapes and sizes."

"Are all these people outside members of the orchestra, then? There seem to be a great many of them."

"No, sir. Not all of them. That was an additional complication. During the course of the events which I have endeavored to describe, and before even I had arrived upon the spot, a certain amount of infiltration had taken place."

"To put it shortly, a lot of people had got in who had no business to be there?"

"To put it shortly—yes, sir. You will appreciate, sir, that the great majority of the orchestra are local ladies and gentlemen, and they all had husbands and wives and so forth in the hall who naturally came round to see what was up and how—" the constable's prose style recovered itself with a visible effort—"how their respective relatives were faring."

"I see."

"As soon as I was at liberty to do so, sir, I stationed a porter on the door to prevent the ingress of unauthorized persons."

"The what?"

"The ingress, sir. Of unauthorized—"

"Yes, yes, I see. But until then there was no checking—"

"No checking their ingress, sir."

"Damn their ingress!" said the inspector, losing his temper. "It's egress that I'm interested in. No checking whether anyone went out?"

"Precisely, sir."

"Which may prove rather more important to this inquiry than who came in afterwards."

"That is so, sir, now you mention it."

"Never mind," said Trimble, repenting of his momentary loss of control. "I have no doubt you did the best you could in the circumstances, and I shall so inform the Superintendent."

"I am very much obliged, sir."

"I think I should see Mr. Evans next, and this Mr. Sefton you mentioned. Where are they, do you know?"

"I think you will find them in a room adjacent to this one, sir. The rehearsal room, it is called, on account of there being a piano in it. I suggested that they should await you there, so as to be free from interruption. There are one or two others with them, I fancy."

There was a knock on the door, and Sergeant Tate's head appeared.

"The Divisional Surgeon is here, sir," he said. "And the fingerprint and photography squad."

"Send them in," said Trimble.

The little room became suddenly full of busy, purposeful specialists. Trimble gave instructions as to his requirements and then departed, leaving Sergeant Tate in charge. But he did not leave soon enough to prevent his hearing the sergeant remark to the fingerprint expert, "It's no use your trying your blower on that door handle, Bert. It's got the inspector's finger marks all over it!"

"That man wants a lesson," was Trimble's unspoken comment. Oddly enough, it was precisely what Sergeant Tate was thinking at the same moment.

The inspector went at once to the room which had been indicated to him as the rehearsal room. It was in all respects similar to the one he had just left, except for an upright piano against one wall, and two or three music stands in one corner. Three men and a woman were standing uneasily by the table, and a fourth man was sitting hunched up in the armchair.

"I am Detective-Inspector Trimble of the Markshire County Constabulary," he began. "Which of you is Mr. Evans?"

Before Evans could answer, the man in the armchair rose to his feet and came staggering across the room.

"My wife!" he muttered hoarsely. "Where is my wife? I must see her! I want to explain—to tell her—"

Trimble caught him by the arm in time to prevent his collapsing completely.

"Mr. Sefton," he said kindly, "I think the best thing you can do is to go back to your hotel and try to get some rest. You shall see your wife in due course, but just now it is not—not convenient. There is a police car at the door to take you, and this officer will accompany you. Now go along, there's a good fellow."

With surprising meekness Sefton allowed himself to be shepherded out of the room. There was a brief silence before Evans spoke.

"My name is Evans," he said. "This is Mrs. Basset, the chairman of our committee. Mr. Dixon, the secretary. Mr. Pettigrew, the treasurer."

Trimble bowed stiffly. An unimpressionable man in the ordinary way, he found it impossible not to be impressed by Clayton Evans.

"I understand that it was you who discovered the body of the deceased," he began, a trifle daunted by the smoldering eyes that stared down at him through the thick lenses of the spectacles.

"Yes. I did. You will of course require a statement from me as to that. I am entirely at your service. But first if you don't mind, I am a little anxious about my orchestra. They have all had a very trying experience, and the professionals will have trains to catch. It is quite out of the question that any of them could have anything to do with this terrible affair. Wouldn't it be possible to let them go?"

Trimble considered the suggestion for a moment.

"I am in rather a difficulty about the orchestra," he said. "I quite appreciate what you say, but from what I have been able to gather so far, one thing seems clear to me. Whoever was responsible for this crime must have had access to the part of the building lying on this side of the stage. There may have been many people in that position, authorized or unauthorized—I shall have to look into it—but obviously the members of the orchestra were among them. I am afraid I shall have to take statements from each of them, simply as a matter of routine."

"Won't it be sufficient for this evening if you take their names and addresses and let them go?" Pettigrew suggested. He had had some experience of police investigations, and saw the prospect of Eleanor being kept long past midnight while a policeman painstakingly wrote down a series of quite useless narratives. "You can interview them at leisure later on," he added.

"Yes, I could do that. But there is a further little complication. From what I have been told, there was an appreciable time between the discovery of Miss Carless's body and the arrival of the police. It would have been quite possible for anyone to slip out in the general confusion. How can I be certain that all the orchestra are still here?"

Evans for the first time looked rather helpless.

"I don't know," he said. "As a matter of fact, I don't even know them all by sight. They were all here when we played the Mozart. I should have heard the difference if anyone had been missing." He turned to Mrs. Basset. "You know them all, of course."

"Of course," said Mrs. Basset. "I can identify everyone to the inspector. Oh—but I was forgetting—there are the professionals. I don't know them."

"You needn't worry about them," Dixon put in. "I've got the list here. I had to arrange about getting 'em here and back to London again," he explained. He produced a neatly typed list from his pocket, and handed it to Trimble.

"Very good," said the inspector. "Now I think I shall be able to help you, Mr. Evans. Get all your orchestra into one room together, and we will deal with them straightaway."

In a surprisingly short time the combined efforts of Evans and Mrs. Basset had succeeded in separating the players from the interlopers who had mingled with them, and segregating them at one end of the corridor. Pettigrew, rather guiltily, remained in the rehearsal room with Dixon. He had been one of the first to come round to the artists' entrance when he realized that a disaster had occurred, and his intention had been the laudable one of looking after his wife; but he had a horror of crowds, and when he had failed to find her at once he had gladly yielded to Mrs. Basset's appeal to lend support to Evans at an informal and rather grisly sort of committee meeting. Twice before in his life he had found himself involuntarily dragged into the investigation of a murder, and this time he intended to stay out—even if Eleanor were to reproach him later on for his desertion.

Through the half-opened door he could hear the disposal of the orchestra proceeding expeditiously enough.

"First violins!" cried Mrs. Basset. "Miss Porteous!"

"Your name and address, please, miss, and may I see your identity card?" from a constable just outside the door, and Miss Porteous passed on, as the next name was called out. The process reminded Pettigrew of a sheep-dipping he had once attended—and, for the matter of that, some of the violins behaved very much like sheep when it came to such a simple matter as identifying themselves.

When Eleanor's turn came he slipped out and collected her,

thereby earning such credit for appearing when least expected that he escaped the scolding he richly deserved for not having joined her before.

"I'll wait until the end, if you don't mind staying," he said. "From what I've seen of this inspector, he'll only make trouble if he finds I've slipped away without leave."

Fresh police reinforcements had arrived meanwhile, and there were now two officers taking names outside, so that it was not very long before Trimble, Evans and Mrs. Basset returned. Pettigrew noticed that the inspector looked rather worried.

"Well, that's finished," he said. "Only two people missing, which is rather better than I had feared. One of them is Miss Hilliard—a viola player. From what the others said, I think there is no doubt her mother got round early and took her home, but we shall have to check up on that. The other may be more troublesome, as it's one of the professionals, and nobody seems to know anything about him." He extended the list to Dixon. "I can't make this name out," he said. "You've penciled it in above the name originally typed."

Dixon looked at it and bit his lip.

"Good Lord!" he said. "Jenkinson!"

"Where does he come from?"

"Whitsea. I've got his address somewhere." He began to search through his pockets.

"You can always get him through Potter and Fullbright," Pettigrew could not resist murmuring.

At that moment there was an interruption. The sound of an altercation was heard outside, and then an apologetic constable put his head into the room.

"Excuse me, sir," he said. "But there's a gentleman outside who insists on coming in. I told him your orders were that nobody was to be admitted but—"

The door suddenly opened wide and a high-pitched voice from without said, "Is this place a concert hall or a lunatic asylum, I should like to know? I tell you, I am *going* to get in!"

And get in he did, in spite of all the officer could do to prevent him.

"Ah!" said Trimble coolly. "And who may you be?"

"My name," said the newcomer, "is Jenkinson. And perhaps you'll tell me what the devil's been going on here?"

8

Jenkinson

Pettigrew, who was the nearest to the door, found his eyes level with the middle button of a dark blue overcoat. Looking upwards, he finally arrived at a thin, pale face with an angry and contemptuous expression, surmounted by a mane of white hair. His first reaction to the sight was that this was about the tallest man he had ever seen outside a fairground; his second, that at all events he had never set eyes on him before.

Jenkinson's question had evidently been a rhetorical one, for without giving anyone a chance to reply he went on to speak in a voice which Pettigrew had little difficulty in recognizing as the one he had heard on the telephone that afternoon.

"I come over from Whitsea," he said bitterly, "at some considerable personal inconvenience, in order to oblige Mr. Evans. I am met at the station by a lunatic or a practical joker—and I am not sure that that is not a distinction without a difference—who drives me to a dance hall in the wrong town and then abandons me. And when finally, by unheard-of efforts, I contrive to make my way to the right place in the right town, I find it entirely occupied by a horde of policemen who dispute my right to be there. I am aware that mine is an overworked, underpaid and generally

71

maltreated profession, but there are limits—and I badly want the blood of whoever is responsible."

Having so delivered himself, Jenkinson deposited a small black instrument case upon the table and favored the company with an unexpectedly good-humored smile. He had, apparently, succeeded in talking himself into a comparatively good temper again.

"And I should add," he went on, "that I shall expect to be paid my full fee and expenses in any event."

"This," said Trimble quietly, "is extremely interesting."

"I am delighted to hear it," replied Jenkinson, looking down on the inspector as from a mountaintop. "Although I am bound to say it falls a long way short of a complete explanation of this extraordinary occurrence. Are you Mr. Dixon, by any chance?"

"I am Detective-Inspector Trimble of the Markshire County Constabulary, and I am in charge of the horde of policemen you were referring to just now."

"I am happy to make your acquaintance. May I ask what brings you here? I can hardly believe that all this police activity has been occasioned merely by my failure to arrive here on time."

"I have reason to believe that a murder has been committed here," said the inspector.

"I see. That explains the fact that the concert for which I have an engagement appears to have been abandoned, though not the extraordinary mismanagement which prevented my fulfilling it. It is not Mr. Dixon who has been murdered, by any chance?" he added hopefully.

"No. Mr. Dixon is here," said Trimble, indicating him. "The person whose death I am inquiring into," he added hastily, before Jenkinson could speak, "is Miss Lucy Carless."

"I am sorry to hear it," said Jenkinson gravely. "I have in my time prayed for the sudden death of a good many concert soloists, but Miss Carless was not among their number. She was a great artist. Well," he picked up his bag again, "I shall not intrude any further on your work. The sooner I am back in Whitsea the better. Mr. Dixon can make such explanations as he sees fit in writing,

72

and my agents will render my account in due course."

He was making for the door when Trimble stopped him.

"Just a moment, Mr. Jenkinson," he said. "I understand you to say that you have only just arrived?"

"That was what I have been endeavoring to convey."

"You were to have taken the part of—" he consulted the list of professional players in his hand—"of first clarinet?"

"Yes."

"When were you engaged?"

"Only this afternoon. I was spoken to on the telephone, first by an ignoramus called Grew, or some such name, and then by this man here, Dixon. I was told positively—"

"Never mind about that. The point is that, contrary to my information, the orchestra was short of one player at the opening of the concert."

"No!" Both Dixon and Pettigrew spoke at once.

"I don't understand," said Trimble, turning to them. "If Mr. Jenkinson was not there—"

"But that's just the point," Dixon persisted. "He *was* there—or rather, the man I thought was Jenkinson was there. I had never seen him before, of course, but I assumed it was him. A first clarinet was there, anyway."

"That is perfectly correct," said Pettigrew. "I was on the lookout for him, as we had had so much trouble in getting hold of a player. He came in just as the National Anthem was ending."

"And it was not this man?" Trimble pointed to Jenkinson.

"Nothing like him," said Dixon.

"Do you agree, Mr. Pettigrew?"

"Absolutely."

"Mr. Evans, what do you say?"

Evans shook his head. "I am afraid I can't help you there," he said. "I couldn't possibly recognize anybody at that distance. But I can say that the wood wind struck me as sounding rather thin during the playing of the National Anthem. What Mr. Pettigrew says would account for that, of course."

"Perhaps you noticed this man, Mrs. Basset? You were in the orchestra, and so nearer to him than anyone else here."

"I should be the last person to see what was going on in the back of the orchestra," said Mrs. Basset, virtuously. "Naturally, I had my eyes on the conductor the whole time."

"That applies to me too," added Eleanor.

"It comes to this, then," said the inspector. "If these two gentlemen are right"—he indicated Pettigrew and Dixon—"there was someone in the orchestra, playing the part of first clarinet, who had no business to be there."

"There's no question about being right," Dixon put in. "Mr. Jenkinson is fairly conspicuous, and this fellow was quite different. He was about half his size, for one thing."

"Very good. Accepting your story, then, we find that this unknown person came on to the stage after all the other members of the orchestra were in their places—and left the building immediately after the murder had been discovered."

"You mean—" Mrs. Basset began, but Trimble held up his hand.

"Finally," he said, "he was only able to effect his appearance in substitution for Mr. Jenkinson because the real Mr. Jenkinson had been unexpectedly delayed on his way to the City Hall."

"Through a piece of remarkable incompetence on the part of my driver," Jenkinson interjected.

"Was it incompetence?" Trimble retorted. "If this man intended to take your place in the orchestra it may well have been part of his plan to see that you did not arrive and spoil his game."

"I don't quite see how he could have had any part in having Mr. Jenkinson delivered to the wrong place," said Pettigrew. "We arranged from this end for him to be met by one of Farren's cars. The driver must simply have made a mistake."

"If it was Farren's car that met him," said the inspector. "However, we can very quickly check up on that. What time did you order it?"

"Some time after five," said Dixon. "I put the call through myself."

"Five ten, to be precise," Mrs. Basset added. "I was there at the time, and my watch is particularly reliable." Anybody who questioned the accuracy of Mrs. Basset's watch, her manner indicated, would be a bold man indeed.

"One moment," said Trimble. "I will have this matter of the car looked into at once."

Leaving the room, he went into the passage and spoke to the constable at the door.

"Ask Sergeant Tate to come here at once, please," he said.

At that moment the sergeant appeared from the artist's room.

"We have finished in there, sir," he reported. "May the body be removed now to the mortuary?"

"Yes."

"Very good, sir. And may I—"

Trimble cut him short.

"You are to go at once to Farren's Garage in the High Street," he commanded. "Find out if they received an order from Mr. Dixon to meet a train at Eastbury and to bring a gentleman to the City Hall this evening. What car they sent, name of driver, and whether the order was carried out. Get a statement from the driver, if possible, and all relevant details. Report back here to me as quickly as possible. Sharp, now!"

Grumbling something under his breath, which fortunately for the inspector's peace of mind was inaudible to him, the sergeant departed. Trimble returned to the rehearsal room. He found Jenkinson impatiently looking at his watch.

"This watch, Inspector, though not particularly reliable," he said, "informs me that it is getting fairly late, and I have not very much time if I am to get any food before I catch the last train back to Whitsea. Since I hope it is now definitely established that I did not reach this place in time to kill Lucy Carless, may I be allowed to go now?"

"I am sorry, sir," said Trimble, "but before you leave I am afraid I must ask you to tell me exactly what happened to you this evening."

"I thought I had sufficiently described that already," said Jenkinson wearily. "Through an inexcusable blunder—"

"No, no. From the beginning, please, and in as much detail as possible."

"Very well. At about five o'clock, then, I was telephoned to by Mr. Dixon and asked to come here to take the place of a clarinetist who had refused to play at the last moment. At least, that was what I gathered had happened, but I may be wrong. It was arranged that I should catch the six thirty-five train from Whitsea and be met at Eastbury Junction at seven twenty-nine. I did catch the six thirty-five and I did arrive at Eastbury at seven twenty-nine, or as near to that hour as makes no matter. And," added Jenkinson firmly, "I was met."

"What sort of car was it?"

"Just a car. There was nothing remarkable about it—except perhaps that it was rather cleaner and more comfortable than is usual. It was the only one waiting at the station, and as soon as I approached the driver opened the door and said, 'Mr. Jenkinson?' I said, 'Yes,' got in, and he drove off."

"What did the driver look like?"

"I really can't tell you. It was dark by then, of course, and the British Railways are fairly economical of their lighting at Eastbury. He had a peaked cap on, and a dark overcoat, I remember. He was a perfectly ordinary man, just like anybody else, and he spoke in a perfectly ordinary voice. Naturally, I took no particular notice of him. I very much doubt if I should know him again."

"You didn't notice the number of the car?"

"As a matter of fact, I did, but that comes later in the story. Since you are interested, you had better have all the facts in their proper order. As I was saying, the man drove off. We drove some distance, but as I am unfamiliar with this neighborhood I cannot say exactly how far, or in what direction. Eventually we reached a

76

town which I assumed in my ignorance to be Markhampton. The car stopped outside a large building, at a door labeled 'Artistes' Entrance.' I got out. No sooner had I done so than the car drove away. I looked after it in some surprise, as I rather expected that the driver would expect a tip (which I was perfectly prepared to add to my expenses account) and at that point I noticed its registration number."

"What was it?" Trimble asked.

"TUJ 104. And should you ask me why I happened to make a note of it, the answer is that I was brought up by a highly disagreeable uncle whose names were Thomas Uriah Jenkinson, so that the initials were unpleasantly familiar to me. As for the number, I can only say that it immediately occurred to me that if my uncle had lived to be a hundred and four he would still be alive and presumably more disagreeable still."

"Thank you, Mr. Jenkinson. Your statement has been extremely valuable. There should, at any rate, be no difficulty about tracing the car now. Where did you find yourself, by the way?"

"I found myself where the car left me—on the pavement outside the Artistes' Entrance. I duly entered, and was presently confronted by a pasty-faced young man in a dinner jacket who demanded to know what I was doing there. I told him that I was a member of the orchestra, at which he looked somewhat surprised and said that he thought the band was all there already. He went away and returned with a creature prominently labeled 'Master of the Ceremonies,' from whom I learned that I had strayed into a Home Guard Reunion Ball at the Assembly Rooms in Didford Parva."

Jenkinson paused at this point to glare fiercely at Pettigrew, who had been seized with an uncontrollable desire to laugh. When order had been restored, at the risk of apoplexy on Pettigrew's part, he cleared his throat and went on.

"To add insult to injury, the fellow suggested that I should, as he put it, 'join the boys' and take part in, and even add to, the hideous riot of cacophony which had by then broken out in another part of the building. After disabusing him of this idea, which was not easy, I set about looking for a conveyance to bring me here. There appeared to be no cars to be obtained in Didford Parva, and I was eventually reduced to waiting in a queue of rustics for the local omnibus, which finally brought me to the door of this police-infested place. That is my story, sir, and if its recital has been as valuable as its experience was distressing, it should rank as the most important piece of evidence ever recorded. Have I your leave to go?"

Whether or not Jenkinson's purpose had been to exasperate the inspector to the point where he would be only too thankful to get rid of him was a question on which one at least of his audience could not be certain. If so, he had succeeded in his plan, for the words were no sooner out of his mouth than Trimble darted to the door and ushered him out with great courtesy and obvious relief.

Returning to the room, the inspector looked at the little group of men and women. It was apparent that they were all in some degree suffering from reaction after the shock of Lucy Carless's tragic end. Their faces were drawn and tired. Mrs. Basset was openly yawning. Evans, hunched on the piano stool, was contemplating the keyboard as if longing to escape from the squalor of events into his own private world of music. Not out of any particular sympathy for them, but because in their then condition they did not seem likely to be capable of giving him much further help, he decided that it was high time to release them.

"I do not think I need keep you here much longer," he said. "Mr. Evans, I suggest that you should come round to the police station, say in an hour's time, when you have had a little refreshment, and I can then ask you to clear up a few points which I want further information about. As for you other ladies and gentlemen, I have your addresses, and I can call on you tomorrow if necessary. I have plenty to do tonight," he added, lest anyone should think that he, Inspector Trimble, was seeking to spare himself. "Before you go, however, there is one question I must ask.

There is one person unaccounted for in this affair, and that is the man who impersonated Mr. Jenkinson, as a player of—what is the name of the thing?"

"A clarinet," said Dixon.

"A clarinet—precisely. Now is this an uncommon sort of thing?"

"Good clarinets are hard to come by, like everything else nowadays," murmured Evans, as though speaking to himself. "I saw a nice B flat one for sale in London the last time I was there...."

"I mean, are there many people about who can play it?"

"A full orchestra has at least two, and a military band a great many," said Evans, coming out of his abstraction. "But if you mean, many people in this neighborhood who can take the first clarinet's part in a piece like Mendelssohn's Violin Concerto, there aren't. That was our trouble."

"Good. That narrows the area of our search a good deal. Last question: What did this particular player look like?"

The question was directed at Pettigrew. He had seen it coming for some time, and was ready with his answer.

"I haven't the least idea," he said.

"What?"

"I'm sorry, but I really haven't, although I was looking out for him, because I was anxious to see if he would arrive in time for the start of the concert. But the light was bad for me, and of course I wasn't looking at him as a person, but just as an item in the orchestra. If he had been a striking figure, like Mr. Jenkinson, I should have noticed, of course. But he wasn't. He was just—well, an ordinary man. He had horn-rimmed spectacles, I can say that, and I rather think he had a mustache, but I won't be sure."

"Tall? Short? Dark? Fair?"

"Middling height, I should imagine, and darkish. But really, he might have been anybody, so far as I was concerned. Perhaps Dixon, you noticed—?"

But Dixon, when appealed to, was equally unhelpful. He had been at the back of the hall, he explained, and his view was, if anything, worse than Pettigrew's. He confirmed the horn-rimmed spectacles, and was fairly positive about the existence of the mustache, but that was as far as he could go.

Trimble shrugged his shoulders.

"Very well," he said. "Perhaps in time I shall find somebody else who was rather more observant. And now, I think—Yes? What is it?"

It was Sergeant Tate, hotfoot from Farren's Garage, holding a hastily prepared report, which he handed to the inspector with an air of satisfaction.

Trimble contemplated it with an air of distaste.

"I can't read this," he said and handed it back.

"I shall have it properly typewritten in due course," said the sergeant breathing heavily. "But seeing that you were in such a hurry for it—"

"Very well, very well. Just tell me the gist of it now, and get it into proper shape later."

Tate produced an old-fashioned pair of steel-rimmed spectacles, wiped them slowly and placed them on his nose.

"'Statement of Wilfred Farren, aged forty-six, National Registration Number, DNEA 335,'" he read. "'I am the owner of the business known as Farren's Garage and Hire Service, 252, High Street, Markhampton. In consequence of a telephone message purporting to come from Mr. Dixon received by me at five twenty this evening—'"

"It was five ten by my watch!" protested Mrs. Basset, indignantly.

"That is what he says, Madam."

"Well, he's wrong. My watch is particularly—"

"Go on, Sergeant," said Trimble.

"'I ordered my employee, John Foch Dawkins, to take one of my cars, registered number RUJ 762, to Eastbury Junction to meet a Mr. Jenkinson by the train arriving there at seven fifty-nine. The car left—'"

"What train did you say?" asked Dixon.

"The seven fifty-nine, sir. 'The car left my garage at—'"

"But I said seven twenty-nine. The seven fifty-nine would have got in too late for the concert."

"'The car left my garage at—'"

"Never mind about the rest of the statement, Sergeant," said Trimble. "I think we have got all we want from Mr. Farren."

"Very good, sir. 'Statement of John Foch Dawkins, aged thirty-one, National Registration Number—'"

"I don't want to hear it. Well, Mr. Dixon, that clears up one part of the mystery, at any rate. We know now why Farren's man failed to meet Mr. Jenkinson. You are quite sure you said the seven twenty-nine?"

"Positive."

"There is no doubt. I heard him myself," Mrs. Basset added. "Farren has become very careless. A man who cannot even keep his clocks accurate is not fit to be trusted. I shall not recommend my friends to employ him in future." Mrs. Basset herself, she indicated, was never reduced to using hired cars in any event.

On this note the meeting terminated. But it was not quite the last observation made that evening bearing on the case. The inspector and the sergeant had driven off in their police car, and the Pettigrews, Dixon, Evans and Mrs. Basset were standing at the stage door of the City Hall before going their respective ways home, when Evans suddenly remarked:

"There's one member of the orchestra who hasn't been accounted for."

"Who's that?" Dixon asked.

"That damned fellow Ventry. Where on earth is he?"

9

Interview with an Absentee Organist

Ventry, in point of fact, was at home. He was sitting at ease in a deep armchair in his music room before a blazing wood fire and smoking a cigar. Such attention as he was able to spare from his cigar he was devoting to the study of a catalogue of choice wines and spirits shortly to be offered for sale by auction by a firm in the City of London. The remains of his solitary cold supper were on the table in the middle of the room. Presently he was roused by the ringing of the telephone.

"Billy?" said a woman's voice.

"Yes."

"Are you alone?"

"Yes. The cook's out."

"I wasn't thinking of cooks, exactly," the voice said, with the suspicion of a chuckle, and then immediately became serious again. "Look here, I suppose you know what happened this evening?"

"Meaning?"

"About Lucy."

"Yes." Ventry was silent for a moment and then repeated, "Yes.

I know about Lucy. It's a bad show, altogether," he added.

"Of course it's a bad show," said the voice. "But that's not what's worrying me just now. It's us."

"I don't quite see where we come in."

"Oh, for God's sake, Billy, be your age! Don't you see it means that there are going to be all sorts of questions asked about this business?"

"Yes. I can see that all right."

"Well, all I want to say is this: If anybody asks you anything about tonight, *you haven't seen me.*"

"I follow," said Ventry. "I haven't seen you. Is that all?"

"Is that all?" The voice sounded puzzled. "Look here, I haven't time to say any more now. I may be interrupted any minute. So long as that's understood."

"You've left it a bit late, haven't you?" said Ventry, grinning maliciously into the mouthpiece of the telephone. "Or perhaps you haven't put your clock right yet? How do you know the police haven't been round here already?"

"Good Lord, they haven't—!"

"No, it's all right, they haven't. But they might have, for all you knew. If you couldn't trust me to hold my tongue, why didn't you ring up an hour ago?"

"Because I've had a parcel of chattering idiots in the house ever since I got back. Besides, I couldn't be sure you were at home. Where were you, anyway, when—I must stop now."

The line went dead abruptly. Ventry stood for a moment, holding the silent receiver in his hand, an expression at once sly and thoughtful on his face. Then he replaced the instrument and walked back to the fireplace. He took his watch from his pocket and compared it with the clock on the mantelpiece before settling down in his chair again. This time he did not pick up the catalogue. Instead he sat idle, his hands on his knees, staring at the fire, while his half-smoked cigar extinguished itself in the ashtray. He looked as though he were waiting for someone—or something.

Inspector Trimble and Sergeant Tate arrived at Ventry's door about a quarter of an hour later. The door was opened to them by the master of the house, who apologized for the absence of a servant to receive them and led them into the music room, where he apologized again for the untidiness of the room, and offered them cigars, which were refused. After these preliminaries the inspector came to the point without further delay.

"I understand, Mr. Ventry, that you were a member of the orchestra at the concert at the City Hall this evening?"

"Certainly not. I was a soloist. Should have been a soloist, perhaps I should say."

"Should have been—precisely. Mr. Evans informs me that you were not there when the concert was due to begin."

"Unfortunately I wasn't. I'm afraid it must have upset Evans very badly, but I thought he would have forgotten it in the greater upset later on."

"Where were you?"

"When? At eight o'clock, when the concert started? I can't say, precisely, but somewhere on the road between here and the City Hall, looking for a taxi or anything that would get me there. I found a bus eventually."

"What caused the delay, Mr. Ventry? You possess a car, do you not?"

"I certainly do, and I intended to use it. I had allowed myself twenty minutes to get down to the Hall from here. But unfortunately the self-starter has a habit of seizing up rather badly from time to time and I found myself stranded."

"I see. And when did you arrive at the Hall?"

"I didn't take the time, but it was too late to be of any use. As I came up to the stage door I could hear the Mozart symphony in full blast. I knew then that Evans had given me up for lost and turned the program upside down. I felt pretty sick about it, I can tell you."

"What did you do then? You went into the Hall, I suppose?"

"No, I didn't. I thought of going round to the front, but Evans

84

never lets anybody in between the movements of a symphony, so that was no good. I could have hung about at the back, I suppose, but it seemed a pointless thing to do. Besides, I badly wanted a cigar, and there's some idiot regulation about not smoking behind the stage. So I just lighted up and mooched around outside. It was a fine evening and I wanted to cool down a bit."

"You are quite sure, Mr. Ventry, that you did not enter the stage door?"

"Quite sure. You can ask the man on the door if you like. I saw him there, though I don't suppose he noticed me."

"It didn't occur to you to go and have a chat with Miss Carless?"

"It did not," said Ventry with emphasis. "Evans had given strict instructions she wasn't to be disturbed, and she is—was—pretty temperamental. I didn't want to muck up two numbers on the program."

"Very well. You mooched around, as you put it, until—when?"

"Until the symphony was over. By that time I had finished my cigar and I was beginning to feel chilly. I thought I might as well go in and listen to the concerto from the back. So I slipped in—the doorkeeper wasn't there then, by the way—and waited. There was quite a longish wait and I expected the concerto to start—but it didn't. I was just going to pop out to see if Evans had decided to take the Handel next after all, when there was a general hubbub and the next thing I knew the place was swarming with the orchestra. I twigged from what I heard that there had been a disaster, so I decided that poor old Handel had had it for that evening and nipped off home as quick as I could."

"By bus?"

"Er—yes, by bus."

"It comes to this, then," said Trimble. "Nobody, so far as you know, can verify where you were while the symphony was being played. But I suppose that there are other members of the orchestra who can confirm that you were there when the concert was abandoned?"

"I'm not so sure of that," replied Ventry, as unperturbed as ever. "You see, I'd made a pretty bad fool of myself that evening, and let the side down good and proper. I wasn't too keen to face the music—or face the musicians, rather—and I was particularly anxious not to meet Evans. You may not believe me, but I'm quite scared of that man sometimes. So to cut a long story short, when I heard them coming, I hid."

"Hid? Where?"

"In the Gents. It's just inside the stage entrance, you know. I shut myself up inside one of the good old Vacant-Engaged compartments, and from there I heard what had happened from the chat of two of the pros who came in on their lawful occasion. Pretty callous they were about it, too. When the coast was clear I just slipped out—and believe it or not, everybody was so busy arguing and gossiping that I don't think a soul spotted me."

"You came quietly home and had your supper as though nothing had happened?" asked Trimble, nodding towards the table.

"I came quietly home and had a drink," Ventry corrected him. "My woman laid this before she went out, which would be six-ish, I expect, and I ate it when I came back here after the rehearsal. Slack of me not to have cleared away and washed up, I suppose, but I don't believe in keeping a dog and barking myself."

"I see," said the inspector. "So you came back here between the rehearsal and the concert. Did you use your car for that?"

"Oh, yes. She was functioning all right then."

"Didn't you leave your car outside the door, if you intended to drive down to the City Hall after supper?"

"Yes, of course, I did."

"It's not outside now."

"Lord, no. I put it away when I got back. The self-starter was perfectly O.K. then. Funny the way these things behave. The car's in the garage now. You can have a look at it if you like."

"I don't think that will be necessary," said Trimble. "Just one other question: How long do you suppose the concert had been in progress when you arrived?"

"They hadn't got very far into the first movement of the symphony—say five minutes."

"Thank you. I think that covers all the matters I wished to ask you about, Mr. Ventry." He glanced at Sergeant Tate. "Is there any point you had in mind, Sergeant?" he asked.

Tate looked up from his notebook. "I think I have all the particulars here, sir," he said. "Just one routine matter, to make the report complete—what is the make and number of this gentleman's car?"

"Since you wish it, Sergeant," said Trimble with a faintly superior smile, rising from his chair as he spoke. "Perhaps you would answer the question, Mr. Ventry?"

"It's a fourteen horsepower Hancock, and the number is TUJ 104."

Inspector Trimble sat down again with a jerk.

"Did you say TUJ 104?" he asked faintly.

"Yes. Why not?"

Trimble stared at him. Ventry stared back without a hint of fear or suspicion visible on his face. If his expression conveyed anything it was merely a slightly mocking good humor, which embraced also Sergeant Tate, whose eye Trimble was careful to avoid. It was an appreciable time before the inspector recovered himself. Then he said:

"If your car was immobilized outside this house from the time you returned from the rehearsal until twenty minutes to eight this evening, can you explain how it came to be at Eastbury Junction at twenty-nine minutes past seven?"

Very deliberately Ventry took another cigar from the box at his side, pierced the end and lighted it.

"I wonder," he murmured as he threw away the match, "what the hell it was doing there." Then he turned a candid countenance to the inspector. "I'm afraid I told you a silly sort of lie just now," he observed easily. "At least, it wasn't precisely a lie, but it had just the same effect. My self-starter *does* seize up from time to time and I *was* stranded this evening. Only the two things aren't connected. So far as I know, the self-starter has been in perfect order all day. What happened was that when I came out of the house, to drive down to do my stuff at the concert, the car simply wasn't there. That's why I was late."

Tate and Trimble both began to talk at once. Trimble got in first with, "If that is true, why on earth didn't you say so at once, instead of telling this cock-and-bull story?"

"Because I felt such an ass," said Ventry calmly. "Besides, I didn't think you'd believe me."

"Did you report the loss to the police station?" the inspector asked.

Sergeant Tate, not to be denied any longer, said in the same breath, "I thought you said just now that the car was in your garage at this moment."

Ventry looked quietly from one to the other before deciding which to answer first.

"I didn't report the loss in the first place," he said, "because I was in such a tearing hurry to get down to the City Hall. I was late as it was, and telephoning would only have made me later. I didn't report it afterwards, because, as this gentleman reminds me, it is at this moment in my garage. And that," he added, "is why, as I said just now, I didn't expect you to believe me."

"Mr. Ventry," said Trimble in a menacing tone, "this is a serious matter, and you may put yourself in a serious position by trying to mislead the police. Please be good enough to tell me the truth without any further beating about the bush."

"Right," said Ventry, leaning back in his chair and pulling at his cigar. "Forget all I said just now about the self-starter. That was simply eyewash. Everything else I've told you about this evening is perfectly true. But you can add this. When I got to the City Hall I noticed out of the tail of my eye a fourteen horsepower Hancock parked just beyond the stage-door entrance. Of course there are scores of them about and it never entered my head that it might be mine. After all, one wouldn't imagine that anyone would pinch my car just to go to the concert. Anyhow, I was in much too much of a hurry to stop to investigate. The only thing that occurred to me was that it was a damn silly place to leave a car, right in the fairway, where it would block everything trying to get out of the car park. But when I found I was too late for the concert, and started to stroll round, I went over to inspect, and by gum! it was my car all right—door not locked, ignition key in the slot, exactly as I'd left it. Well, I thought, that saves me and the police a bit of bother, anyway. So I got in and sat there while I finished the cigar. When the symphony was over I went back into the Hall, as I told you, but I locked the door this time to make sure the blighter who had brought it there wouldn't take it away again. Then, when I came to make my getaway, I nipped back into the car, started up just in time—there was someone hooting behind for me to get out of the way already—and buzzed off home. That's what happened—and if you don't believe me, all I can say is, I warned you."

There was a long pause when he had finished.

"So that was what happened, was it?" said Trimble at last.

"Yes."

"Can you play the clarinet, Mr. Ventry?" The question was shot out abruptly. If it was intended to take Ventry by surprise it certainly succeeded. For the first time he looked thoroughly taken aback.

"The clarinet?" he repeated. "Well, as a matter of fact I can—or could once, rather, because I haven't touched it for years. But for God's sake don't tell anyone. Why do you ask? Oh, by the way," he went on, without waiting for an answer, "there was rather a mess-up at the rehearsal over a clarinetist who walked out. I thought that had all been put right, though. Has that anything to do with it?"

"I'm not here to answer questions," the inspector replied sternly. "But for your information, Mr. Evans has told me what occurred at the rehearsal. Why do you not want it known that you can play this instrument?"

"Because I hate it like poison," said Ventry simply. "It's like

89

this. My father—God rest his soul—was mad about chamber music. He started with trios—he played the fiddle and my brother was quite a useful cello. My mother had to take the piano, though really she was a better violinist than he was. Then, as soon as my sister was old enough to make some sort of noise on a viola, it was quartets, with poor mother as second fiddle of course. But that wasn't enough for the old sinner. One day he took it into his head that the family ought to tackle the Brahms Clarinet Quintet, so at a ridiculously early age I was sat down to learn the beastly instrument, when he knew perfectly well all I cared for was the organ, and I'm allergic to Brahms, anyhow. Damn selfish, wasn't it?"

"Very interesting," said Trimble, dryly. "But that still doesn't answer my question."

"Why I've kept quiet about being able to play the thing since I've lived in this place? Well, that's obvious, isn't it? If I let on that I could, I should have Evans at me to turn out for every one of his concerts. Or perhaps he didn't tell you of the wood-wind shortage that comes up at every committee meeting? It's a standing dish. No thanks, I'd much rather keep quiet and pay for a pro to do the job—it's only a drop in the bucket of what I do shell out for the orchestra every year, anyway."

"Do you possess a clarinet?"

"Rather. I've got quite a nice set—B flat, A, and E flat. Lovely things they are, too—it's only spitting into them myself that I object to."

"May I see them, please?"

"Yes, if you like. I don't care what you do—so long as you don't expect me to play them."

Ventry rose, and led the officers to the hall of the house. Large, glass-fronted showcases lined both the walls. They were full of musical instruments of all kinds, at which the inspector gazed with complete lack of comprehension.

"A regular museum you've got here," he observed.

"Quite a nice collection," said Ventry complacently, throwing back the doors of one case. "Actually my uncle made it. Funnily enough, he couldn't play a note of anything, but had a passion for buying old instruments. I've just added a few things from time to time. I picked up that theorbo only the other day, for instance. But of course the gem of the collection is—"

"There's a clarinet in the corner," observed Tate, interrupting him without ceremony.

"What? Oh yes—rather a nice piece, that. Over a hundred years old. I don't suppose it has been played for years. The key system is quite different from the modern type, as you've noticed, no doubt."

"I've noticed nothing of the sort," snapped the inspector, who was beginning to feel the strain of several hours of hard work coming on top of a normally busy day. "I asked you to let me see your clarinet, the one you can play when you're so minded, and I wish you'd do so without beating about the bush."

"Sorry!" said Ventry equably. "I forgot you weren't an enthusiast. The chaps you're looking for—and I still haven't the foggiest idea why—are down here, on the bottom shelf. Now which do you want to—Hullo! That's damned queer!"

"What is queer?"

"The B flat's missing. It's funny. I could have sworn I saw it here yesterday."

"What's a B flat? Is it part of the instrument you mean?"

"Certainly not. I mean that one of my clarinets has gone."

"Which one?"

"I tell you—the B flat."

The inspector gave it up.

"Whichever it is," he said, "tell me this. Is it the one you'd have taken to play in the concert this evening, if you had been playing the clarinet and not the organ?"

"Yes, I should think so. You'd better check the scoring with Evans, though. But I don't understand—"

"Never mind whether you understand or not," Trimble interrupted. "The point is—the instrument has gone."

"I understand *that*," said Ventry suavely.

"Since yesterday?"

"I'm pretty sure it was here yesterday."

"What makes you sure?"

"Well, I had a little party here yesterday to meet Miss Carless and her husband—or rather to meet Miss Carless. The husband was a sort of compulsory extra. They were here before the other guests arrived and I remember showing them my collection. We had all the cases open and I took out some of the best things for them. I'd have been bound to notice if the B flat had been missing then."

"Suppose I were to tell you, sir, that I have reason to think Miss Carless was murdered by the man who played first clarinet in the orchestra this evening?"

Ventry raised his eyebrows and then said slowly, "I don't know what the answer is to that one, Inspector. But if you mean what I rather think you do, I can only say this: if there's one thing I should be less likely to do than to commit a murder, it would be to play that damnable instrument in public."

10

Interview with a
Bereaved Husband

It was nearly midnight when the two detectives returned to their headquarters, but Inspector Trimble showed no signs of going to bed. Sergeant Tate watched him, with a growing sense of grievance, as he sat at his desk, ploughing steadily through the pile of reports and statements that the case had already produced. Tate was concerned not so much with the lateness of the hour—policemen, like seamen, are schooled to dispense with sleep when the occasion demands—as with his superior's manner of dealing with him. For this was the time of night, and the stage in the investigation of a case, when his former inspector would light his pipe, take down his back hair and gossip endlessly, deliciously, as man to man; weighing the pros and cons in his slow, measured tones, heavy with the familiar Markshire accent, inviting his assistant's views and making him feel that the officers of the Markhampton Force, whether they got their man or not, were friends and brothers, irrespective of rank. Not so the New Bloke. He did not even smoke. Just sat there like a graven image, reading his papers and looking clever. Showing off, Tate reflected bitterly; that was the only word for it—showing off.

When Trimble finally looked up from his reading it was merely to fire off a curt question.

"Who did I send to take the statement from the stage door-keeper?" he asked.

"Jeffrey," said Tate briefly. That was another grievance. Jeffrey was one of these smart-aleck young detectives whom the inspector favored, and he had been detailed to do a bit of real work, and perhaps get some real credit, while a man of seniority and experience like himself was left to tag along behind the great Trimble like a little dog.

"Ah, yes, Jeffrey." Trimble found the statement and read it in silence.

The sergeant could not resist observing: "The doorkeeper says that he left his post for five minutes just before the concert was abandoned. He says he went to talk to the man on duty at the main entrance about some eggs he had promised him. Actually what that young man's interested in isn't eggs at all but clothing coupons."

Trimble looked up from his reading long enough to remark, "That doesn't make much difference, does it? The point is that he wasn't there."

"Which may have been very fortunate for somebody," said Tate. But if he had hoped to draw the inspector out he was disappointed, for that maddening person only grunted, and began to gather his papers up into a neat pile.

Tate made one more effort.

"Mr. Ventry's housekeeper didn't notice the car in the drive when she left the house this evening," he said. "I particularly asked her—"

"She also said that she left by the back way," retorted Trimble. "You may not have noticed that there is quite a substantial hedge between that and the front door. I verified myself that you can't see over it, and she's a short woman."

He stood up. "Tomorrow," he announced, "we will call at the hotel for Mr. Sefton at ten A.M. and take him to the mortuary for the formal identification of the deceased. After that will be the time to take a full statement from him. The Chief has arranged for a conference at noon. Good night."

Sergeant Tate went home a sulky, dissatisfied man.

"This inspector has got his ideas all wrong about the case," he confided to his wife, as he undressed for bed. "Dead wrong, from start to finish."

"Why, what are his ideas, exactly?" asked Mrs. Tate innocently.

"I'm damned if I know," her husband confessed. "But mark my words, Flo, they're wrong, whatever they are!"

At a quarter to ten the next morning a car left police headquarters for the Red Lion, which, as every visitor to Markhampton knows, is the principal hotel in the city. Inspector Trimble had advanced the time for their departure by ten minutes, though characteristically he had not troubled to tell the sergeant his reason for doing so. The explanation came when, on arriving at the hotel, Trimble, instead of making his presence known to Sefton, sent for the headwaiter and engaged him in ten minutes' close conversation. Reluctantly, Tate admitted to himself as he listened to their colloquy that the inspector could see as far through a brick wall as the next man.

The waiter was then despatched to find Sefton, and the little party set off immediately to the mortuary. The bereaved husband stood the grisly ceremony well. He was pale and calm, though the unnatural rigidity of features suggested that he kept himself under control with difficulty. When it was over the inspector said to him:

"I shall want a brief statement from you, sir, for the coroner. That will save you a lot of time and trouble at the inquest, when you come to give your evidence there. Just a formal matter, of course. Perhaps if you would care to come round now to the police station ..."

Sefton came and was installed in a comfortable armchair. He was given a cigarette from the box kept by the inspector for the use of visitors less abstemious than himself, and generally treated with a blend of deference and sympathy that exactly suited the occasion. It was, Tate conceded, a very pretty setup altogether—if you liked that way of going to work.

"Let me see, Mr. Sefton," Trimble said, his fountain pen playing busily over the statement form before him, "have I got your full Christian names? And the address?...Thank you. Better have the number of your identity card while we're about it.... Thank you very much. Now we can start: 'I am the husband of'—What was your wife's full name, Mr. Sefton?...Really! Funny the names these foreigners give their children, isn't it?—'husband of Lucille Olga Sefton, professionally known as Lucy Carless.'—Is that correct, sir? I don't want to put down anything wrong, because of course this is your statement, and I shall ask you to sign it in a moment.... Right! I'll go on: 'I was married to my wife on—' When was it exactly, sir?...Dear me! As recently as that! How very tragic! Now then: 'At ten fifteen A.M. on Saturday the fourth November...I attended at the mortuary, Corporation Street, Markhampton, where I was shown the body of a woman, whom I identified as my wife. She was aged—' How old was your wife, sir?...Quite so—'aged thirty-five, and had hitherto enjoyed good health.' I take it that is so, sir?...Quite. 'I last saw her alive at—' When would you say you last saw your wife alive, Mr. Sefton?"

"About half-past seven last night."

"Half-past seven," repeated Trimble, continuing to write. "That would be at the City Hall, I take it?"

"Yes. We had gone there together from the hotel. I left her in the artist's room."

"You left her alone?"

"Yes. She always wished to be left alone before playing in public. It—it was a matter of temperament, you will understand."

"You mean, you came with her to the Hall, saw her into her room and came straight away?"

Sefton shifted uneasily in his chair. Insensibly the atmosphere of the interview had changed. The questions had ceased to be

96

merely formal, though at what point they had done so it was difficult to say.

"Er—yes, I suppose so," he muttered.

"I only want to ascertain if I can who was the last person to see your wife alive," said Trimble. His voice was reassuring, but he had laid down his pen. "Now from what Mr. Evans tells me there must have been quite a lot of people about behind the stage at that time, and I wondered—"

"I've just remembered," Sefton put in. "I didn't go straight away. I stayed with my wife ten minutes or so, talking."

"I quite understand. Were you talking about anything in particular, Mr. Sefton?"

"Oh no. There was nothing special—just this and that."

Trimble did not pursue the matter.

"I see," he said. "Then it would be roughly twenty minutes to eight that you left?"

"Yes. I can't pretend to be accurate, of course, but—"

"No, no. Of course not. One can only be approximate in such matters. And you went round to the front of the house, I suppose?"

There was an appreciable pause before Sefton answered.

"No. As a matter of fact, I did not."

"Not? But surely you had been given a seat for the concert?"

"Yes, I had, of course. For the first half of the concert, that is. I was accompanying my wife in the latter part. But I decided to go for a stroll outside instead."

"Decided to go for a stroll," the inspector repeated. He sat silent for a moment as though to let the phrase sink in. Then he looked across the desk directly at Sefton and said softly, "That was an unusual sort of thing to do, wasn't it?"

Sefton avoided his eye. He looked more uncomfortable than ever. "I suppose it was," he said. "But there were some things I wanted to think out."

"Things connected with music, perhaps?" Trimble suggested helpfully.

"Yes, that's it," Sefton agreed a shade too eagerly. "My wife and I weren't quite in agreement about the interpretation of one of the pieces we were going to play that evening, and I wanted to work it out in my head without being distracted. It's a technical point and perhaps you wouldn't understand—"

"No," said Trimble dryly. "Perhaps I wouldn't. Would that be the subject of the conversation with your wife during the ten minutes you were in the artist's room with her?"

"Yes. Oh, yes."

"You didn't say so just now when I gave you the opportunity. Did you have a meal at the hotel with your wife before you left for the Hall, Mr. Sefton?"

"Yes, I did. But I don't see—"

"From what the headwaiter tells me, your disagreement with her on that occasion was not on technical points of music."

Sefton's face had suddenly become a dark, angry red.

"No," he said. "It was not. It was on a personal matter."

"Personal to you two, or involving some other person?"

After a brief silence Sefton broke out, "It's not a subject I wish to discuss. My wife is dead. She had her faults, like everyone else, and I was not always as patient with her as I should have been. Can't we leave it at that?"

"I'm afraid we can't, Mr. Sefton," said the inspector smoothly. "You see, the evidence in my possession indicates that you and your wife that evening had something in the nature of a quarrel, in which some other man's name was mentioned. Surely you must see that I have to investigate this business, if only in your own interests. Frankly now, sir, what terms were you on with your wife?"

Sefton flung out his arms with an air of desperation.

"How on earth can I make you understand?" he said thickly. "Have *you* got an attractive wife?"

It was the inspector's turn to be taken aback.

"Have *I*—?" he faltered.

"Of course you haven't! Not attractive in the sense that Lucy was. How can *you* know what it means to be married to a woman who is so made that she attracts every man she sees; who isn't satisfied to earn her living by making an exhibition of her beauty and talent to a crowd of goggling imbeciles, but encourages—yes, *encourages* every nasty creature who comes near her to—to take liberties—" His voice broke on something that was nearly a sob.

Trimble drew breath to speak, but before he could say anything Sefton had begun afresh.

"Isn't that something to quarrel about, as you call it?" he demanded. "Wasn't I justified in warning her where her conduct would lead to?"

"Do you mean that her death was due to the conduct you have been speaking about?" Trimble interposed quickly.

"What else could it have been? She tempted fate once too often and this was the result. It was madness letting her come here in the first place and I ought to have known it."

For once in a way the inspector at this point felt positively grateful for the presence of Sergeant Tate. The interview which he had managed with such skill up to now was bidding fair to run away from his control altogether. The solid, bovine form of Tate, making notes at the side of the desk, was a reassurance of normality now that he was fairly certain he had to deal with a man on the brink of hysteria. In a deliberately matter-of-fact tone he said:

"Why was it madness to bring her to Markhampton in particular? I should have thought it was a pretty safe place, on the whole."

Sefton's face assumed a look of crazy cunning. "Markhampton's full of people who knew my wife well," he said. "Knew her a lot too well, if you ask me—had known her years before I had—that's a nice thing for a husband to put up with, isn't it? Evans, to begin with—he's known her ever since she came over from Poland. Ventry, too—she'd known him in London before he got his house here—how would you like to trust your wife with a man like that? She swore to me she'd never met that old man Pettigrew before, but d'you think I'd believe her? They were talking for minutes on end at Ventry's party, as though they were old friends. And as if that wasn't enough and more than enough, she goes out of her way to meet and smile at and talk to Dixon— *Dixon* of all men! Do you know who Dixon is?" he suddenly asked.

"I understand he's the secretary of the orchestra," said the inspector, in some surprise.

"He is the former husband of my wife. Now do you understand?"

"I can quite see that meeting him may have been rather awkward, but after all—"

"Awkward! Awkward! My God! Can't you realize that it was hell? I warned her of the danger she was running into, but she would take no notice."

"What danger are you referring to exactly, Mr. Sefton?"

Sefton laughed wildly. "'What danger' is good," he said. "Here is a woman killed and you ask what danger was she in!"

"I did not ask that," the inspector pointed out. "I asked you what danger you warned her she was running into by meeting these gentlemen you have mentioned—and Mr. Dixon in particular."

Sefton did not reply for a moment. He sat silent, breathing fast, his fingers drumming on the arms of his chair.

"I should have thought it was obvious," he said at last, in a calm, flat voice. The excitement seemed suddenly to have oozed out of him, and he looked tired and almost apathetic.

"It seems very far from obvious to me," remarked Trimble. "I can understand an attractive woman being in danger from—from someone who claimed the right to be jealous of her attentions to other men, shall we say? Why should she be in danger from her divorced husband? I should have thought he was the last person to have any motive to harm her."

Sefton said nothing.

"Are you sure that was the kind of danger you warned her of, Mr. Sefton? Or was your warning in the nature of a threat of what

100

you might do if she was too friendly with other men?"

Color rushed into Sefton's face.

"No, no!" he exclaimed, with a touch of his former vigor. "I tell you I loved my wife! I wouldn't have touched a hair of her head!"

"Very well." The inspector abruptly closed the discussion and resumed again in a matter-of-fact tone. "You were saying that you left the Hall at about seven forty and went for a stroll. Where did you go?"

"I don't know. Nowhere in particular. I just walked up and down. I didn't go far from the City Hall for fear of losing my way."

"And you came back—when?"

"About half-past eight, I suppose. I was aiming to get back well before the interval, so as to see if my wife wanted to run through any of our pieces in the second half of the program. When I got back I was surprised to hear no music going on, as the concerto should still have been playing at that time. I thought my watch must have stopped. I went in by the stage door. I saw nobody about, so I walked straight into the artist's room. Evans was there and a doctor. They—they told me ..."

The sentence trailed away miserably.

"Quite," said Trimble. "But can you give me the name of anybody you saw or spoke to during the fifty minutes or so that you were outside the building?"

Sefton shook his head slowly.

"I don't think—" he began. Then his face cleared. "Yes," he said, "I remember speaking to someone."

"Oh? And who was that?"

"I have no idea."

"You really mean to say you spoke to somebody and don't know who it was?" asked the inspector incredulously.

"How the devil should I know?" retorted Sefton. "I had plenty on my mind that evening. I tell you, this was just a man in the street I passed a casual remark to. I never gave him a second thought."

101

"It might be to your advantage to remember something about him," said Trimble dryly.

"Well, I can't. I just have a vague recollection of talking to a man, and that is all. Wait a minute, though.... I believe—I have a distinct impression that he was in a uniform of some sort."

"Was he a policeman?"

"No—no, I'm fairly certain he was not a policeman."

"Very well. If I may give you a piece of advice, sir, you would be wise to take steps to find this man in uniform who is not a policeman as soon as possible. If you can," he added, pointedly. "And now, sir, I'll just get your statement in order and you can read it through and sign it."

Sergeant Tate cleared his throat violently.

"Did you want anything, Sergeant?" asked Trimble in his most superior tone.

"Yes, sir. I should like to ask this gentleman if he can play the clarinet."

"No," said Sefton at once, "I don't and I can't. Why do you ask?"

Neither officer replied to the question. But Trimble looked at Tate and said quietly, "Thank you, Sergeant." And whether he was being sarcastic or not, Tate could not in the least determine.

11

A Conference with the Chief

Though he had never admitted it to anybody, even to himself, Inspector Trimble was a little afraid of his Chief Constable. It was not that the Chief was a particularly awe-inspiring personality, or a stickler for discipline. On the contrary, he was a quiet, unassuming man, on the best of terms with most of his subordinates. Personally, Trimble had nothing whatever against Mr. MacWilliam, who had trusted him, promoted him, assisted him in every way. But there was none the less, barely perceptible, something in the Chief Constable's manner towards him which never failed to induce in him a certain feeling of nervousness. He seldom criticized, his suggestions were always helpful and to the point, his behavior was invariably courteous and considerate. The real trouble, as Trimble finally came to realize, was that he never seemed quite to take his detective-inspector altogether seriously. The work—yes. Nobody could complain that MacWilliam did not regard that as serious. A more devoted police officer never existed. But through and above the work itself, during their gravest conferences together, Trimble was disturbed and secretly intimidated by the consciousness that he himself was under scrutiny—a scrutiny none the less searching for being quite kindly—and that the scrutineer was gently amused by what he saw.

Like everyone else, the inspector had his private creed—articles of faith which, once perhaps the subject of argument, had long since become part of his very nature, too firmly embedded there to be questioned or disturbed without the risk of damage to the whole fabric. The Chief Constable's attitude struck at two of them simultaneously—the article that laid down the essential worth and importance of Detective-Inspector Trimble and the one that decreed that whereas he, Trimble, was gifted with an acute and lively sense of humor, nobody whose name began with a Scottish prefix could possibly see a joke. Small wonder that before this double assault on the citadel the garrison should feel fear.

Notwithstanding, it was with every outward sign of confidence that the inspector, with Sergeant Tate at his heels, walked into the Chief Constable's room shortly after the interview with Sefton had been concluded. He found him, as usual, sprawling at ease behind a large desk entirely bare of papers. Mr. MacWilliam's first action on being appointed Chief Constable of the county had been to abolish the tray marked "Pending" which had ornamented the desk since time immemorial. His simple system was to dispose of every matter as it reached him and then to pass straight on to the next. He contrived to combine this rule with a rigid adherence to the day's timetable by a capacity for concentrated work which his quiet and rather casual manners entirely belied.

"Well, Inspector," he began, "I thought I'd better have a chat with you and Tate about this Carless business. I skimmed through the papers you sent me this morning and it looks a bit troublesome—quite a bit troublesome. I take it you have been pretty busy?"

"Very busy indeed, sir," said Trimble.

"I've had a word with the coroner, and I gather that the inquest is fixed for tomorrow. I presume that you will be applying for a formal adjournment?"

"Yes, sir. We shall not be in a position to carry the matter any further tomorrow."

"Quite. And what exactly is the position? I'd like you just to run over the case as far as it has gone, if you don't mind."

Exposition was not Trimble's forte. On paper his style was lucid and direct, avoiding with almost ostentatious care the stilted officialese of the ordinary police report. But when it came to explaining himself by word of mouth he found himself continually slipping into the worn phrases which he had picked up in his impressionable youth, and which modern educationalists have taught us to despise. His efforts to avoid them, and to find acceptable substitutes, reduced him from time to time to fits of stuttering incoherence. These were not improved by the kindly assistance of Sergeant Tate, who was always ready in an emergency with the very cliché which he was anxiously trying to dodge. By the time that he had finished, under MacWilliam's quietly appraising eye, the sweat was pouring down his cheeks.

"Quite," said Mr. MacWilliam. He said nothing else for an appreciable time, but remained leaning back in his chair with his hands in his pockets, his gaze wandering round the ceiling of the room, his full lips rounded as though at any moment he might give vent to a whistle. "There are several odd features about this case," he said at last. "Let me see if I can sort them out. I dare say you have done so already, Trimble"—here his mild blue eyes looked suddenly into the inspector's own, with an expression of complete seriousness. But *was* he as serious as he looked? Trimble asked himself with an anxious qualm—"but it would help me to run through them once more—if you don't mind, that is. First point: Miss Carless has a row with Zbartorowski at the rehearsal. This results in the orchestra being short of a clarinetist. Second point: Jenkinson is engaged in his place and a car is ordered to meet him at the station, but that car goes to meet the wrong train and misses him. Third point: The car that does meet Jenkinson belongs to Ventry, and the driver, whoever he is, takes him to the wrong place, so keeping him out of the way until after the murder. Fourth point: Ventry fails to turn up at the start of the concert, so that the order of events on the program has to be changed. Fifth point: Somebody does play the clarinet part in the orchestra and that somebody disappears immediately after the murder is discovered. All these are plain facts, which don't depend on the evidence of anybody who could conceivably be described as a suspect. Am I right so far?"

"Yes, sir," said Trimble.

"They may not all be of equal importance, they may not all be connected with this crime—it's just possible that none of them are—but take them together, they're a damned odd set of facts which call for a bit of explanation."

"I agree, sir, and my explanation—"

"So you have an explanation, Trimble? That is excellent! An explanation that will fit all five points, I presume?"

Trimble felt uneasily that he had stumbled into a trap. He considered for a moment.

"No, sir, not all of them," he admitted. "But it doesn't follow that all of them are connected, as you said just now."

"It's a good working principle to prefer the hypothesis of a single origin for a correlated set of phenomena to that of the fortuitous coincidence of two or more," said the Chief Constable, a strong trace of Scottish accent appearing in his voice for the first time. "I'm not sure if I am word perfect," he added apologetically, "but that, or something like it, was what I was taught in my student days. In other words, if these things aren't connected with each other, and with the sixth and most important point, which is the crime itself, there's been a most unnatural amount of rum goings on over this concert. Take them in order: If Zbartorowski had not refused to play at the concert, Jenkinson would not have been sent for; if Farren's car had met the right train, Jenkinson would have played at the concert; if Ventry had arrived at the City Hall in time to perform his piece on the organ, his car would not have been available to maroon Jenkinson at Didford Parva, and Jenkinson might still have got there before the concert began.

All these things had to happen just as they did before the unknown clarinetist could take his place in the orchestra, and if the unknown had not done that—well, it's reasonable enough to suppose that we shouldn't be discussing this case now. What do you think, Tate?"

Sergeant Tate, unexpectedly appealed to, took his time before answering. He shook his head slowly, swallowed twice and then observed, "It seems to me a regular House that Jack Built, sir."

"A very, *very* good description," said Mr. MacWilliam with emphasis.

"Thank you, sir," replied the sergeant modestly.

Trimble was torn between contempt for Tate's obtuseness and envy for the simplicity that could accept such a compliment.

"My explanation," he said doggedly, "doesn't deal with the first point, I grant you that, sir. But I don't see that any explanation needs to. After all, the fact that the orchestra was short of a clarinet may have been just a fluke—the bit of luck that gave the murderer his chance. Suppose the whole plan to kill Miss Carless only originated after the rehearsal—took its starting point from that, in fact?"

"Very well, I'm prepared to grant that. What follows?"

"I look at it this way, sir. We are looking for a murderer who can play the clarinet. Ventry can, though nobody in the orchestra knows it. They are expecting him to take his place in the organ loft, and he doesn't. Nobody expects him to turn up in the orchestra, and in any case none of them are looking that way at the critical time. The audience isn't a bit interested either, except for two of them—Mr. Dixon and Mr. Pettigrew—and I wouldn't give two pins for their evidence on identification. With the simplest disguise, or no disguise at all, he could have slipped in at the back of the stage and nobody been any the wiser. He says his car was taken from outside his house—I don't believe him! I think he drove it to Eastbury Junction, ditched Jenkinson at Didford Parva and came back to the City Hall just in time to kill Miss Carless while the National Anthem was being played. That deals with all the points that matter, sir, and what's more it gives you a hypothesis of a single whatyoucallem so far as the order of the concert being upset is concerned, if you follow me, sir."

The Chief Constable, who had listened with attention, nodded slowly in reply. "Yes," he said, "ye-e-e-s. You put your point very—very forcibly, Trimble. But you don't seem to me to have covered point two."

"Point two, sir?"

"The fact that Farren's car went to meet the wrong train."

"Well, that may have been just coincidence, sir. It made things easier for Ventry, I admit. But I don't see why he may not have gone to the station to catch Jenkinson just the same. If he got there in good time and hung about at the entrance and asked for Jenkinson as soon as he appeared, ten to one he'd pick him up under the nose of a hired driver who'd wait till he was looked for."

"That would be taking a bit of a risk," Mr. MacWilliam objected. "And talking of risks, I don't quite see why he should have bothered to go through all this business, which simply had the effect of drawing attention to his own absence from the organ loft. Assuming he arrived at the City Hall just in time to kill Miss Carless while the National Anthem was being played—the noise would drown any sounds of a struggle from behind the stage, I suppose—why not go straight up to the organ and play his piece as he was expected to?"

"Perhaps he didn't feel equal to playing the organ right after committing a murder," the inspector suggested.

"You may be right there, but—you were about to say something, Sergeant?"

"I was only going to call your attention to the recorded case of George Joseph Smith, sir," said Tate.

"Thank you, Sergeant. That is most valuable. Although the argument from analogy is apt to be fallacious. Besides, Smith didn't give a concert performance after he had drowned the lady in her bath but merely played for his own delectation. No—there is something else about points two and three that troubles me a good deal more. Did Ventry know that Jenkinson was expected by that particular train? Did he know that Jenkinson was expected at all? Because if he did not, the whole theory, with the greatest respect to you, Inspector, seems to me to fall to the ground."

"Well, he must have, sir, mustn't he?"

"Must have, Trimble? I'm not sure that I follow you."

"Because if he didn't know, he couldn't have planned to take Jenkinson's place."

"I see that we are in agreement after all. You put the point differently to myself, but it comes to the same thing," said the Chief Constable politely. Trimble, feeling vaguely that he was being "got at," shifted uneasily in his chair. "Now, as I understand the position," he went on, "Ventry, according to his own account, at any rate, came straight home after the rehearsal had been interrupted, and did not leave his house again until he was due to drive down to the concert. But Jenkinson was not engaged for the concert until some time after that, and Farren's car was ordered later still. That was done by Mr. Dixon over the telephone, I remember, and several people were present at the time. Surely Ventry was not among them?"

"I'll check that up to make certain, sir," said Trimble. "Somebody might have told him about it, though."

"With what object? Deliberately? If so, we have got to look for an accomplice."

"That seems very likely, sir," the inspector said. "I'm glad you've suggested it. I've thought all along that this was a very complicated business for one man to have worked by himself. Look here, sir, how about this? The accomplice rings up Ventry's house and tells him the arrangement. Ventry then gets on to Farren's and alters the train to be met so as to make sure their car won't get to the station in time to meet Jenkinson. There was some question about the exact time when the message was sent, I remember. Then he carries on as I suggested just now. That explains everything."

"Excellent, Trimble, excellent!" said the Chief Constable with a warmth that was none the less a little suspect to the inspector's suspicious mind. "I knew you would have an answer to my doubts. Now it only remains to prove that Farren's received two messages and not one—and to find the accomplice," he added.

"I'll go and see Mr. Farren again," said Tate. "Perhaps he did have more than one message, though he certainly didn't mention it last night."

"Do so, Sergeant. That will clear up one point, at any rate. As to the accomplice, I shall leave that side of the inquiry in your very capable hands, Trimble. It should not be too difficult to find out who was present when Mr. Dixon telephoned to Farren, so that will narrow the field a good deal."

"Very good, sir."

The Chief Constable had tilted his chair back once more and was regarding the ceiling with an exploratory eye.

"We seem to have spent rather a long time considering the case of Ventry," he remarked. "But I have no doubt you have considered all the other possibilities."

"Yes, sir," said Trimble, "I have." His voice sounded a little sulky, as it was apt to do after he had endured a long exposure to his superior's good humor. He had provided a perfectly sound solution to the affair and the Chief had admitted that it was a good one, subject to the verification of some minor details. Why couldn't the man leave it at that?

But MacWilliam was evidently determined not to leave it at that. Apparently drawing inspiration from the picture rail, which he was now studying with intense concentration, he began to speak at about twice the pace of his previous utterances.

"Suppose—just suppose—Ventry's story is true," he said, "—and you will, of course, Inspector, have considered the desirability of checking it so far as is possible—trying to trace the conductor of the bus that took him to the City Hall, finding anybody who passed his house between, say, six o'clock and seven forty-five and saw or did not see his car in the drive, and so forth and so on—suppose it is true, where does that leave us?"

Without waiting for an answer he went on, more rapidly than ever, "It leaves us with a number of possibilities, does it not? Sefton, for example. Is it possible that he may simply have killed his wife before he left the hall, and all this clarinet business be simply a monstrous concatenation of circumstances which has some other explanation and no connection with the crime at all? Have we any proof that she was alive after the time that he went for his walk? Alternatively, can we really be sure that he is telling the truth when he says that he can't play the clarinet? We shall have to make inquiries in London as to that. If he can, then he might have taken Jenkinson's place, although he obviously could not have had the time to drive to Eastbury and back by way of Didford. That would entail an accomplice again, who was familiar with the arrangements made for meeting Jenkinson. Then, failing Sefton and Ventry, we are still left looking for a man who can play the clarinet. Where's Zbartorowski, to start with?"

This was a question to which an answer was obviously expected and Trimble was ready with it.

"I had not overlooked the matter of Zbartorowski, sir," he replied rather stiffly.

"I didn't for one moment think you would, Trimble," said MacWilliam politely. "I just asked, that's all."

"I caused inquiries to be made at his lodgings last night and again this morning," said Trimble. "He has not been seen there since yesterday morning."

"I see. Well, that may be significant or it may be not. Meanwhile, if you can't get in touch with him quickly, I suggest you could consult Mrs. Roberts."

"Mrs. Roberts, sir? Do you mean the lady that plays the viola?"

"Is that what she plays? I mean the one who is on the committee of the Music Society, anyway."

"I should hardly have suspected Mrs. Roberts, sir."

"I'm not suspecting her of anything. I only know that I went to tea with her one Sunday a month or two ago, and Zbartorowski was there. I gathered that she had taken him under her wing, in the way she does. She introduced me to him, and I never saw a man look so scared in all my life. Have we anything against him, by the way?"

"Nothing definite, sir, but I'm pretty sure he's been operating in the black market in a small way."

"Well, that ought to help you to pick him up."

"There's something just occurred to me, sir," Sergeant Tate put in. "If Zbart—if this Polish fellow played at the concert, wouldn't he have been recognized by the fellow who sat next him? After all, he had been at the rehearsal."

"Quite right, Sergeant—unless he had disguised himself in some way. Get in touch with that man, whoever he was—Mr. Dixon can supply his name and address, I suppose—and let him have a photograph of Zbartorowski, and of Ventry. Oh yes, and of Clarkson, too. He might be able to recognize one of them."

"Clarkson, sir?"

"Yes—I was coming to him. He's our next clarinetist on the list. Don't you recollect, in Mr. Evans's statement he says that it was necessary to engage two players because the only amateur available, one Clarkson, was not good enough to take the first part and wouldn't play second?"

"That is correct, sir. He did say so, though it didn't seem relevant to me at the time."

"It probably isn't relevant, but if we're looking for a man who knows how to play a particular instrument it doesn't do to overlook anyone who can. I should recommend you, Inspector, to investigate Clarkson."

"I will, sir," said Trimble resignedly.

"Those are the only two players we know of, I fancy. Now, is there any chance of our being able to find a crypto?"

"I beg your pardon, sir?"

"I mean, another man like Ventry, who can really play the thing but doesn't let on that he can."

"I should think it very unlikely, sir, so far as the Music Society is concerned. All the playing members were actually in the orchestra at the time of the crime, apart from Ventry, of course. The only nonplaying members of the committee are the secretary and the treasurer—Mr. Dixon and Mr. Pettigrew. I shouldn't think that either of them—"

"Neither should I, but just to be on the safe side you may think it worth while to make sure." MacWilliam looked at his watch. "That seems to be as far as we can go for the time being, Inspector. Is there any other point you wish to mention?"

"I don't think so, sir. We are, of course, conducting a search for Mr. Ventry's missing clarinet and making the usual routine inquiries to try to trace the origin of the stocking with which the murder was committed."

"Yes. With you, Trimble, I am sure I can take such things for granted. By the way, this is not a case in which you feel you would like some assistance?"

"Assistance, sir?" said Trimble, bristling.

"From Scotland Yard, I meant."

"No, sir," said Trimble firmly. "I'm not asking for any help from the Yard."

"Very well," said the Chief Constable politely. "I just thought I'd mention it."

At five minutes to one Mr. MacWilliam, punctual as always, went out to his lunch. The inspector watched him go from the window of his office. Before him was a sheet of scribbled notes. They ran as follows:

> Who was present when Dixon phoned Farren?
> Did Farren get one message or two?
> Conductor of Ventry's bus.
> Anyone else who saw Ventry's car.
> Was deceased alive when Sefton left?
> Can Sefton play clarinet?
> Find Zbartorowski—consult Mrs. Roberts.
> Find professional clarinet in orchestra.
> Find and interview Clarkson.

Get photographs of Ventry, Zbartorowski and Clarkson.
Can Dixon or Pettigrew play clarinet?
Trace stocking.
Ventry's clarinet.

"That seems to be as far as we can go for the time being,
Inspector," he murmured with bitter irony.

12

Lunch at the Club

On the day after the concert Pettigrew went to lunch at the Mark-shire County Club. On coming to live in Markhampton he had thought it his duty to become a member of that respectable insti-tution whose solid, unassuming premises are familiar to everyone whose business or pleasure takes him through the Market Square. He did not make as much use of his membership as he had expected, possibly because his domestication had proved more thorough than he had believed possible, but it gave him a certain standing among the worthies of the county besides offering a use-ful refuge on the occasions when, as happens in the best regulated marriages, home became momentarily untenable. This was such an occasion, Eleanor having decided to pay one of her rare visits to London.

The shabby, comfortable dining room was more crowded than usual and he was relieved to be able to find a table to himself. Everybody in the room was, naturally enough, intent on the same topic of conversation, and it was a topic which he felt peculiarly anxious to avoid. He was not abnormally squeamish, he told him-self, but he found it impossible to enter into a discussion about the murder of Lucy Carless with the relish that his fellow members were so cheerfully displaying. Murder in the newspapers was interesting enough—a welcome distraction from the far more somber and depressing news that seemed to monopolize the bulk of the papers nowadays. Murder as the subject of a brief, neatly typed out and tied up with pink tape with a decent fee attached, was a matter for self-congratulation and a godsend in a lean term's work. Murder in the raw—murder of a charming woman whom one had met and liked and chaffed over her distaste for Dickens not forty-eight hours since—that was a different thing altogether. It simply didn't bear thinking of. If only one could avoid thinking! Pettigrew had made up his mind at the earliest possible stage that this time he was not going to allow himself to be drawn into the inquiry which, reason and experience told him, had already begun and was even now proceeding at the highest possible pressure into every ramification of the affair in the hands of highly trained experts. Twice before, by the merest chance, he had stumbled on something that had helped to uncover a crime. He had not enjoyed either experience. This time there was nothing he could conceivably know or do that would afford the police the smallest help. This sober, comforting conviction made it all the more irritating that he could not, try as he would, shut his mind to the whole business. Instead he found his thoughts recurring over and over again to the events of the last two days, on the wild suspicion that somewhere, at some time, he had seen or heard something that it might be his duty to disclose to the authorities. It was a quite irrational suspicion, he told himself, merely the product of his pity for the dead woman and the shock of having been so closely concerned with the circumstances of her death; but it persisted in spite of himself. It was time that he gave it its quietus. Deliberately shutting his ears to the hubbub of conversation going on around him, he unfolded *The Times* which he had brought with him, propped it against the water jug on his table, and set himself to read the Births, Deaths and Marriages with unwonted concentration.

"Do you mind if I share your table?" said a pleasant, low-pitched voice.

Pettigrew nodded without speaking and kept his eyes fixed upon his *Times*. But before he had reached the foot of the column his natural good manners had asserted themselves. After all, this was a club, and not a public restaurant, and he did not wish to acquire the reputation of a curmudgeon. He removed the paper from its improvised stand and looked across to the newcomer with as pleasant a smile as he could muster.

It was with mixed feelings that Pettigrew realized that he was confronting the Chief Constable. His first reaction was one of disgust. MacWilliam's mere presence served to recall to his mind the very subject which he was deliberately trying to avoid. But second thoughts brought relief. He knew the man only slightly, but it seemed fair to suppose that a person in his position would be the very last to wish to gossip on the matter, and it was gossip which Pettigrew was most concerned to be spared. Glancing round the room, he could see that necks were being eagerly craned in the direction of his table, and he reflected that the Chief Constable had been fortunate—or prudent—in selecting as his table companion the one person who would not seek to pump him on the topic of the hour.

The meal proceeded in silence. MacWilliam ordered his lunch and applied himself to it with seriousness and dispatch. At the other tables the conversation which had been interrupted by his entrance resumed itself, though in a noticeably lower key. Pettigrew began to think, with a feeling of relief in which disappointment was oddly mingled, that he would finish his lunch without exchanging a single word with his neighbor. Then, just as he was spooning into his mouth the last of the tasteless crème caramel which the club almost invariably provided by way of a sweet, the Chief Constable leaned across towards him and spoke.

"D'you mind if I ask you a question, Mr. Pettigrew?"

"No, of course not."

"I've been having a chat with Inspector Trimble this morning, and he'll be at you again, I have no doubt. But meeting you here, like this, I thought I might clear my own mind on the matter, if you have no objection."

When he desired to be particularly ingratiating MacWilliam allowed a certain Scottish lilt, too faint to be called an accent, to color his phrases. Pettigrew, who was English of the English, found it irresistible.

"No objection at all," he repeated.

"Well then, can you tell me this—you'll recollect, no doubt, Mr. Dixon telephoning yesterday afternoon about Mr. Jenkinson coming to play at the concert?"

"I can recollect only too well," said Pettigrew with a shudder. "Actually, I did a good deal of the telephoning myself."

"But it was Mr. Dixon who ordered the car from Farren's, was it not?"

"Oh, that! Yes, certainly he did."

"Now this is the question: who, so far as you can remember, was present when that was done?"

Pettigrew considered the question carefully.

"Let me see," he said. "I was there myself, of course. Then there was Mr. Evans, Mrs. Basset, and—let me see—I rather think Miss Porteous was there, too."

"Miss Porteous?"

"The first violin. She is a member of the committee, too, you know."

"Quite so. Was there anybody else?"

"I don't think so. But the door of the room was open at the time and I can't be sure if any other members of the orchestra weren't about outside. The rehearsal had just come to an end, you will remember, so they were apt to be all over the place. I wasn't paying any particular attention."

"Can you say whether Mr. Ventry was there or not?"

"I am quite positive he wasn't. He had gone off much earlier, before we had succeeded in getting hold of Jenkinson. He was

118

rather offended, I remember, because Dixon turned down a suggestion of his for a substitute player."

"That would be a young man named Clarkson, I take it?"

"Yes," said Pettigrew in some surprise. "That was the name."

"I see." The Chief Constable lit a cigarette and stared thoughtfully in front of him. Around them the room was emptying, as members went in search of coffee in the smoking room. "Would you mind very much, Mr. Pettigrew, if we had our coffee in here? I have"—he looked at his watch—"a few minutes to spare, and—"

"Not at all, not at all," Pettigrew assured him. All the same, he felt absurdly anxious that the discussion should end as soon as possible.

"Strictly speaking," MacWilliam went on, "I shouldn't be asking you all this, because, as I have said, the matter is in the hands of Inspector Trimble. He is a very—a very conscientious officer" —Pettigrew fancied that at this point he could detect something like a twinkle in the Chief Constable's eye—"and I'm sure you will give him every possible assistance. Perhaps it would help him if, when he sees you, you did not mention that we had met in this way."

"I quite understand."

"I was sure you would. Now, do you think you may have mentioned this telephone message we have been discussing to any other person?"

"I think so—yes. I am pretty sure I told my wife about it."

"About what, precisely?"

"About the whole business of getting hold of someone to take the place of this confounded Pole. I had been worked pretty hard that afternoon and had a rather ludicrous experience talking to Jenkinson when I finally got on to him, and—"

"But did you tell Mrs. Pettigrew or anybody else that you knew that Farren's car had been ordered to meet the seven twenty-nine train that evening at Eastbury Junction?"

"Oh, dear me, no!"

119

"I was afraid not." The Chief Constable sighed, and appeared to be waiting for Pettigrew to say something. He waited in vain for a long moment and then said quietly, "If I may say so, Mr. Pettigrew, you display unusual restraint."

"I don't understand you," said Pettigrew stiffly. He understood perfectly well, and realized at the same time that MacWilliam knew it, and was deriving some amusement from the fact. Strange, he reflected, how expressive an apparently immobile face can sometimes be! This fellow is telling me that I'm a liar as plainly as a man could without batting an eyelid. I wonder how he does it?

"I was referring, of course," the Chief Constable explained elaborately, "to the admirable restraint with which you have contented yourself with answering my questions. Most people would have been unable to resist the temptation of asking what they were all about."

"I have some experience both of asking questions and answering them," Pettigrew could not resist saying.

"Some experience—yes." MacWilliam appeared to be immensely entertained by the admission, though not a muscle of his face moved. "I think you know my friend Mallett of New Scotland Yard?"

"Yes," said Pettigrew, sulkily. He felt that he was being driven into a corner.

"You won't mind my telling you, I hope, that he has a very high opinion of your intelligence?"

It was the last straw. Not the compliment, but the mild, deprecatory tone in which it was phrased, proved too much for Pettigrew's reserve. Suddenly he wanted to laugh out loud, to greet this odd, subtle creature as a man and a brother.

"Tell me, Chief Constable," he said, "do you play chess?"

"I do, a little. And—not to imitate your restraint—why do you ask me that?"

"I was just wondering how many moves ahead you could see."

The two men looked into each other's eyes for a moment in silence and then both began to laugh simultaneously.

"I think we can call the game off, Mr. Pettigrew," said MacWilliam, becoming serious again. "I know what you are feeling about this, but I've a strong idea you can help me. Mr. Mallett has often told me—"

"Is Scotland Yard coming in on this?" Pettigrew asked.

"I think not. I don't want to discourage Trimble on his first big case, and he's a sensitive fellow. I fancy my Force can do all the detection work that's necessary. It's just that I've a feeling that there's something about the case that takes it a little beyond a policeman's depth. And that's where you come in."

Pettigrew nodded. Exactly how he did not know, he found himself taking for granted the very thing he had been rejecting as unthinkable less than half an hour before.

"Of course," MacWilliam was saying, "it's only a feeling. We haven't got all the facts yet—simple little facts like those I was asking you about just now—and it may be that when they are all assembled the whole thing will turn out quite plain. But I don't think I'm wrong." He looked at his watch again and rose from the table. "I must be getting back to my office. You'll want to see all the particulars in the case, of course, so far as they have gone."

"Shall I come over to your place now and pick them up?" Pettigrew asked, rising in his turn. "I have the afternoon free."

"Did I not tell you that Trimble was a sensitive man?" said the Chief Constable reprovingly. "My goings out and comings in are all done under his window. It would break his heart if he knew I was bringing anyone in behind his back."

"Of course—I shouldn't have made such a stupid suggestion."

"I'll be round at your place this evening, say at nine o'clock, and run through the facts with you," MacWilliam went on, as they walked through the deserted dining room towards the door of the club. "That is, if Trimble doesn't take it into his head to come and interview you then. But I'll find out his movements in advance. And you'll not forget, whenever he does come, that so far as he is concerned you are just a poor, dumb witness answering questions."

"Is he likely to ask me any that you haven't asked me already?"

"Well, he is liable to want to know whether you can play the clarinet. You can't, I suppose?"

"Good Lord, no!"

"Do you happen to know of anybody else who can—Dixon, for instance?"

"Dixon is notorious for knowing all about music, while remaining quite unmusical. That's why he's such a satisfactory secretary. I think you can be quite sure he can't play a note of anything."

"I see." The Chief Constable stopped just short of the door. "Perhaps it would be as well if we left the club separately," he said with a conspiratorial air. "The constable in the Square has a way of noticing me when I go past him and if we were together he might mention it to someone."

"By all means," said Pettigrew. "But before you go, if it's not too crude a question, what exactly do you want me to do?"

"Do? Why, I'm not asking you to do anything. All I suggest is that you should read the police reports, keep your eyes open, and do a little thinking about what you've seen and heard and read. And then, if anything occurs to you, just let me know."

"I see."

"The idea being," the Chief Constable concluded, "that if Trimble seems to be in difficulties I can drop him a hint. I'm afraid he finds it remarkably distasteful to accept a hint from me, and it would be downright nauseating for him if he knew that it came from an outsider like yourself. That's why I'm keeping you in the background. I hope you don't mind, seeing what a good cause it's in."

"No," said Pettigrew. "I suppose I don't. I thought I did mind having anything to do with the business, but I find I'm wrong. As you say, it's a good cause."

"The highest possible cause in the world," said MacWilliam solemnly. "The honor and glory of the Markshire County Constabulary."

And, to Pettigrew's surprise, this time he seemed to be completely serious.

13

Polish Interlude

"Mr. Zbartorowski?" said Mrs. Roberts in mild surprise. "But, Inspector, what do you want to see Mr. Zbartorowski for?"

"That, Madam," replied Trimble, "is neither here nor there. I am asking you to assist the police."

Mrs. Roberts looked milder than ever. "But I don't see why I should assist the police," she observed, in the manner of a kind-hearted housewife gently declining to buy unwanted goods from a traveling hawker. "Mr. Zbartorowski is a friend of mine who has had a very hard time, and I want to assist *him*." She picked up the sewing on her lap and recommenced the work which she had put aside on Trimble's entrance, as though to emphasize that, so far as she was concerned, the interview was at an end.

"Are you suggesting, Madam—?" the inspector began, but he did not bother to complete the sentence. It was only too apparent from the serenely obstinate expression on her face, as she sat with her eyes intent upon her needlework, that Mrs. Roberts was in fact suggesting all those unheard-of, barely mentionable things that he was about to put to her. Instead he looked round the room and caught the eye of Mr. Roberts, who sat smoking his pipe in the armchair on the opposite side of the fireplace.

The appeal was not in vain. One had only to look at Mr. Roberts to realize that he was the embodiment of law-abiding respectability. That shining bald head, those healthy pink cheeks, those ample curves beneath his waistcoat betokened sound qualities that simply did not go with any foolish notions of assisting dangerous foreign down-and-outs whom the police wanted to question. He rose ponderously from his chair and stood with his back to the fire, looking down at his wife with kindly condescension.

"I really think you might answer the inspector's questions, Jane," he said. "After all, it is the duty of all of us to come to the aid of the forces of law and order."

"I wish you would not interfere, Herbert," replied Mrs. Roberts, still without looking up. "You know I never meddle in your affairs. You must please let me arrange my own in my own way."

"But dash it all," her husband protested, "when one is dealing with a case of murder—"

"Don't be silly, Herbert," Mrs. Roberts retorted, reaching for her scissors and neatly snipping off her thread. "You know perfectly well Mr. Zbartorowski has nothing whatever to do with any murder. He is not that kind of person at all."

"But my dear girl, nobody has said that he has."

"Then I don't know why you introduced the subject, I'm sure." Mrs. Roberts rolled up her sewing and put it away in her workbag.

"Mr. Roberts is quite right, Madam," Trimble interposed. "I am not suggesting that your friend has committed a murder—"

"—I should hope not!"

"—but at the same time, my instructions are to find him and put to him certain questions which may be of assistance to the police in tracing the murderer."

Mrs. Roberts looked at him. "Are you telling the truth, Inspector?" she asked in a tone of candid inquiry that robbed the question of all its offensiveness.

"Certainly I am, Madam."

"Why didn't you say so when I asked you just now?"

Trimble looked uncomfortable. "I—I didn't conceive it to be my duty to do so," he faltered. "You must understand, Madam, that there are certain regulations to which we have to conform."

"Fiddlesticks," said Mrs. Roberts simply. "I asked you a perfectly simple question and you didn't choose to answer it. However, if you can promise me that you only want to ask Mr. Zbartorowski about this murder, which he hasn't done—"

"Yes, Madam," said Trimble in desperation. "That's what I'm telling you."

"—and not about all the things he has been doing...?" Mrs. Roberts allowed her voice to trail away and looked inquiringly at the inspector. There was a moment's awkward silence, broken by an embarrassed cough from her husband.

"Really, Jane!" he protested. Mrs. Roberts paid no attention to him.

"I'm sure I don't know what you're talking about, Madam," said Trimble stiffly.

"Then you must be a very bad policeman," Mrs. Roberts commented in the same mild tone. "But as I was saying, if that is all you want, I'm sure Mr. Zbartorowski won't mind telling you anything you want to know. I'll go and fetch him."

"You'll—*what?*" Mr. Roberts's pink cheeks had gone a dusky crimson.

"Really, Herbert, I wish you wouldn't interfere. It isn't at all like you. If you don't mind waiting a few minutes, Inspector." She went towards the door.

"But where is this fellow?" Mr. Roberts demanded.

"In the kitchen. He is really a very good washer-up. And he has been cleaning your shoes for the last three days, but I don't expect you have noticed. Housework," she observed, "is such a nuisance when you have no servants, and now the children are away I am really glad of any help I can get. But of course the great thing was to keep him sober and out of mischief, poor fellow."

She was still talking, in her placid, unselfconscious manner, as she trailed out of the room, carrying her sewing in one hand while the other patted ineffectually at her untidy head of hair. Left behind, the two men stood awkwardly on either side of the fireplace, each avoiding the eye of the other. Presently they heard her returning.

"There's nothing to be frightened about," she could be heard saying through the open door. "The inspector has promised me he won't ask you about petrol coupons or things of that sort, and anyway he doesn't know anything at all about them, so it's quite all right. Come along like a good fellow and get it over!"

There was a pause, and then Tadeusz Zbartorowski appeared in the room, apparently propelled gently but firmly from behind, looking more melancholy and more seedy than ever before, and in addition evidently extremely frightened.

"Here he is!" said Mrs. Roberts brightly, following her protégé into the room. "You won't keep him long, will you, Inspector? I've several jobs for him still to do."

Trimble ignored her. He had suffered acutely in his self-esteem since he entered the house and now at last he was back on the familiar territory of official routine where he could be master.

"Tadeusz Zbartorowski?" he asked.

The Pole, looking miserably at his shabby shoes (which Mr. Roberts, had he looked in the same direction, might have recognized as an old pair of his own), nodded without speaking.

"I am Detective-Inspector Trimble of the Markshire County Constabulary. I have reason to believe that you may be in a position to assist the police in their inquiries into the murder of Mrs. Sefton, professionally known as Lucy Carless, on the evening of Thursday last. Would you have any objection to accompanying me to the police station and there making a statement in writing?"

"Oh no!" said Mrs. Roberts, before Zbartorowski could reply. "You've got it all wrong, Inspector. That isn't the idea at all."

"Jane!" protested her husband. "You really must not interrupt again. You've caused quite enough trouble already."

"I don't know what you mean about causing trouble, Herbert. It seems to me I've been extremely helpful. This gentleman wanted me to find Mr. Zbartorowski and I've found him. But I never said anything about letting him be taken off in a Black Maria to the police station. It's a ridiculous idea. If you want to ask him any questions, Inspector, you can do it here, where I can keep an eye on you and see that you keep your promise."

Keeping his temper with some difficulty, Trimble said, "I should prefer, Madam, to interview this gentleman in the ordinary way, at the police station. It would obviously be more convenient."

"It would be most inconvenient," Mrs. Roberts retorted. "I can't possibly spare him in the kitchen just now. Anyway, I don't see that you have any choice in the matter. You asked him if he had any objection to coming to the police station and he has every objection. Haven't you, Mr. Zbartorowski?"

Zbartorowski's large brown eyes turned towards her. He looked absurdly like a meek, devoted spaniel.

"Yes, Madame," he murmured.

"That's settled then," said Mrs. Roberts, with a sigh of relief. She sat down again in her chair and folded her hands on her lap in an expectant attitude. "Now will you begin, please, Inspector? We've wasted a lot of time already."

Trimble acknowledged defeat. As Mrs. Roberts said, quite a lot of time had already been wasted over what should have been a quite short and simple matter, and the best thing now was to get it over and done with. He wondered whether that incalculable man, Mr. MacWilliam, had foreseen the kind of reception he would get at this house and had directed him here in order to gratify his diabolical sense of humor. There was one grain of comfort, at least—he had no witness to his discomfiture. Mercifully, he had sent Sergeant Tate to make the further inquiry at Farren's that afternoon. It would, he felt, have been altogether destructive of discipline to endure such a reverse in the presence of a subordinate.

"Very good," he said resignedly. Turning towards Zbartorowski he resumed his official manner with some difficulty. "You were engaged to play an instrument in the concert at the City Hall, I understand?" he said.

"The clarinet—yes, sir."

"You attended the rehearsal during the afternoon?"

"Yes, sir."

"During the rehearsal there was an altercation between you and Miss Carless?"

"Pardon?"

"An altercation—a dispute. You had an argument with her?"

"It was not a dispute nor a what you called it," said Zbartorowski, coming suddenly to life. "She used bad words to me. She called me a——. I don't know what is the equal of that word in English, but in Polish it is very, very bad. Then she say that if I play in the concert she will no more play, and I say, Thank you very much but if that is so *I* will not play with such a person and then I went away, and Mrs. Roberts here and many, many other persons who was there on the platform will tell you that what I say is true, and Mr. Evans also and Mr. Dixon, who speaks my language, he also will tell you that what this woman said to me—"

"That'll do, that'll do!" With an effort Trimble succeeded in stemming the flow of words. "It's no good running on too fast, you know. I want to know what the trouble was all about."

"Pardon?"

"What was the cause of the dispute?"

"There was no dispute, I tell you. She called me a bad word and then she say—"

"Why wouldn't Miss Carless play with you in the orchestra?"

"Ah, that!" Zbartorowski shrugged his shoulders and was silent for a moment. When he spoke again the animation had died out of his face and his habitual expression of melancholy had returned. "It was personal between me and she, you will understand. Also political. It is not easy to explain."

"Personal?" The inspector caught at the word. "So you had known Miss Carless before?"

Zbartorowski shook his head. "No," he said. "Perhaps when she was a little girl. I do not know. She was not called Carless then, anyway. It is no matter. All that belongs to the long ago—to a Poland that exists no more. You will not want to hear about that."

"I'm quite sure you won't, Inspector," Mrs. Roberts put in. "It's a very sad story, and nothing to do with you."

Trimble resolutely disregarded the interruption, but he did not press the subject any further. "Very well," he said, "so you left the concert hall in the middle of the rehearsal. What did you do?"

"I go out. I wait till the pubs open and then I get drunk. What else have I to do?" said Zbartorowski simply. "Mr. Dixon has paid me some money in advance of the concert, so I can drink."

"Where were you when the concert began at eight o'clock that evening?"

The Pole shrugged his shoulders again. "The Antelope, the Crown, the Black Horse—I do not know," he said. "If you ask them, they will tell you. I was very drunk in all of them that night."

"You are sure you did not go back to the City Hall at any time?"

"Oh, no. How could I? By eight already I was stinking."

"Did you arrange with anybody to take your place at the concert?"

For the first time Zbartorowski permitted himself to smile. "As if I should do so," he said. "This Carless who is so clever, she can play the clarinet herself for what I cared, and the bassoon also. It was nothing to me."

"I see." Trimble paused for a moment, and looked at the other thoughtfully. "And since then," he went on, "you have not been back to your lodgings?"

"No."

"Nor did you turn up on Saturday night to play in the dance band where you have been employed?"

"No." The voice was hardly audible.

"Why not?"

Looking more acutely miserable than ever, Zbartorowski muttered, "Because I can no more play."

"What exactly do you mean by that?"

With the tortured expression of a man confessing to an unforgivable sin, the Pole slowly raised his eyes to meet the inspector's. "I broke my instrument," he said reluctantly.

"Broke it? What do you mean? Did you have an accident with the thing?"

"No, no!" It was the voice of a man in an agony of remorse. "You do not understand! It was no accident! That night, I—Tadeusz Zbartorowski—of the Varsova Opera orchestre—took my clarinet—my own instrument—and smashed it up in the bar of the Antelope pub—so drunk I was—and because I might no more play in Mr. Evans's concert orchestre! And the pieces I give to the barmaid of the Antelope—and she laughed at me, so funny it was," he added bitterly.

To Trimble's extreme embarrassment, large tears were coursing down Zbartorowski's sallow cheeks.

"There, there!" said Mrs. Roberts in a comforting tone. "You had better go back to the kitchen now. Make yourself a good hot cup of coffee and you'll soon feel better."

Casting a look of gratitude at his patroness, Zbartorowski stumbled from the room. Trimble made no attempt to detain him. He had got all that he wanted. Zbartorowski, he felt sure, might now be written off as a serious suspect in the case, though it would be necessary to confirm his story by routine inquiries at the Antelope, the Crown and the Black Horse. Very shortly afterwards he took his leave, glad to be out of a house where he had endured such acutely uncomfortable moments.

He found Sergeant Tate awaiting him when he arrived back at the police station.

"I have taken a supplementary statement from Farren, sir," he said, and laid upon his desk a neatly typed copy.

Trimble glanced through it. It was short and clear enough. Farren was quite positive that on the evening of the concert he had received only one telephone message ordering a car to go to Eastbury Junction.

"Oh!" said Trimble. It required all his self-control to confine himself to that one monosyllable, and he hoped that he had uttered it in a manner calculated to impress the sergeant with his omniscience and self-confidence. But he was by no means sure that he had succeeded.

14

Bluebottle's Progress

"Buzzing about like a bluebottle, the inspector is," remarked Sergeant Tate to his wife, as he left her to go on duty a few days later. "Just like a blooming bluebottle—with about as much idea of where he's going, and about as useful."

It was perhaps an unfair comparison, because in point of fact Trimble's investigations had been by no means fruitless. Working on the list which he had compiled after his conference with the Chief Constable, he had succeeded in clearing up a number of points. Zbartorowski, with the assistance of the barmaid at the Antelope, had been eliminated so thoroughly that it did not seem worth while to get his photograph for submission to his fellow clarinetist in the orchestra. Next, he had painfully extracted the information which, unknown to him, Mr. MacWilliam had already derived from Pettigrew over the lunch table. The number of potential clarinet players was not increased and the mystery surrounding the engagement of Farren's car remained *in statu quo.* He had then gone on to unearth one fact that might be of genuine importance—at least one positive grain of truth to set against the disappointing mass of negatives which was all he had to show so far for his work. The fatal stocking, by a fortunate chance, had been identified, through some technical peculiarity which Trimble did not begin to understand but which was as clear as noonday to the manufacturers, as being one of a consignment delivered during the month of October to Messrs. Chapman and Frith, the one and only departmental store in Markhampton.

So far, so good. But having advanced to this point, the inspector again found himself at a dead end. Chapman and Frith, with the best will in the world, could not assist him further. The stocking that had been destined to choke the life out of Lucy Carless had reached them in a parcel of some twenty dozen pairs, and had been sold together with its fellows over the counter for cash (accompanied, their manager begged to assure him, by the appropriate coupons). The whole lot had gone off in the course of one fervid morning. The assistants at the hosiery counter still shuddered as they recollected the scene when the stocking-starved maids and matrons of Markhampton and the surrounding countryside had stampeded into the shop and cleared the place of the first full-fashioned sheer, superfine nylons that had been seen in the city for many a long month. They could not possibly begin to identify any individual among that eager, clutching crowd, any more than could the constable on duty who had marshaled the waiting queue outside before the shop doors opened.

But at least it was something to know that the thing had been bought locally. Although the fact was not conclusive evidence that the murderer came from Markhampton or the immediate neighborhood, it certainly gave reason for thinking so, and Trimble was not sorry to be able to eliminate the possibility of an outsider in the crime, since it also strengthened his hand in resisting the suggestion that an outsider should be brought into the detection of it. Sergeant Tate, indeed, in his blunt, unscientific manner, remarked as soon as he saw the statement from the stocking manufacturer, "Well, that lets Sefton clean out of it." Trimble thought it his duty to rebuke him for jumping at conclusions, but very shortly afterwards two further morsels of information reached him which convinced him that Tate was right.

134

The first came in the form of a confidential report from Scotland Yard, in response to a request which Trimble had put through immediately after his conference with the Chief Constable. It indicated that whatever other vices he might have Sefton was not what MacWilliam called a "crypto-clarinetist." The Yard reported that discreet inquiries had been made into his musical career. He had studied at the Royal College of Music, where his principal subject had been, naturally enough, the pianoforte. His second instrument there had been the violin and he had left the College without, so far as could be ascertained, having so much as touched a wind instrument. Ever since he had been professionally occupied as a concert pianist and accompanist, and there was no evidence whatever that he had had the opportunity or the inclination to do anything else.

The remaining possibility—that Sefton had disposed of his wife before the concert began—was knocked on the head by Clayton Evans in the simplest possible manner. Trimble went to see him at his rambling, untidy house just outside the city limits and was received courteously enough, but with an air of detachment that he found somewhat disconcerting. Evans seemed, indeed, to have lost all interest in the affair. He had already, he pointed out, made one statement to the police; clearly, he had no wish to be troubled again. But Trimble persisted.

"I want your assistance, if possible, in clearing up one further point, sir," he said. "Who, so far as you know, was the last person to see or speak to Miss Carless before she was killed?"

"I should say that I was," replied Evans casually.

"But surely, sir," the inspector protested, "your previous statement makes it clear that you saw her last when she went into her room in the company of her husband?"

"That may be. But I spoke to her after that, and she spoke to me."

"When?"

"While I was on the way to the rostrum to open the concert."

"Are you now saying, sir, that you spoke to her through the door of her room?"

"Yes. As you know, the artist's room opens on to a corridor running behind the stage. So does the rehearsal room, which I was using. When I was about to go on to the platform I walked along the passage, opened her door a crack and said, 'Are you feeling all right, Lucy?' She answered, 'Yes, thanks, bless you!' or something of the kind. Then I shut the door and came away."

"You have no doubt that it was her voice you heard?"

"Not the slightest," said Evans with finality.

"You never mentioned this incident to me before," said Trimble reproachfully.

"That is perfectly true," Evans admitted. "But on the other hand I don't think you asked me about it."

"Not in so many words, perhaps," Trimble protested. "But surely you must have seen that it was important."

Evans shook his massive head slowly.

"I am not, thank God, what is generally called a practical man," he observed. "I don't pretend to understand practical men. Their values seem to me all wrong. They attribute enormous importance to things which so far as I can see don't matter a damn, and they tend to disregard altogether things which, to me, are obviously fundamental. And the difficulty that I find in dealing with them is that it is quite impossible to tell in advance what they will regard as important and what not. Accordingly I long ago adopted a system, to which I have ever since scrupulously adhered, of taking everything said or suggested by a practical man at its face value, no more and no less. It is the only logical procedure, because the invariable characteristic of practical men is never to look below the surface of anything. When you interviewed me before, you asked me when I last saw Lucy Carless. I gave you a perfectly accurate answer. This time you wished to know who was the last person to speak to her. I have answered that also to the best of my ability. If you think of any other questions I shall do the same. And it is no use," Evans continued as Trimble opened his mouth to reply, "it is no use telling me that I ought to have known that such and such a piece of information

136

was relevant to the inquiry, because I am not a practical man, and so far as I am concerned the whole inquiry is completely irrelevant in any case."

Trimble had some difficulty in keeping his voice under control as he said, "I don't quite understand what you mean by that, sir."

"I mean simply this: that whether you catch anyone for this murder or not, it doesn't make a hap'orth of difference. The only thing that matters is that the next time you want a solo fiddle for a concert it will have to be someone who is not Lucy Carless—and no amount of detecting or arresting will alter that."

After which, there was really nothing more to be said.

Not Zbartorowski. Not Sefton. Neither Dixon nor Pettigrew. The inspector noted, with grim satisfaction, as he crossed off the items on his list which he had eliminated, that all save one of those remaining dealt more or less directly with the man whom, despite the Chief Constable's objections, he continued to regard as the likeliest of suspects. The exception was Clarkson, the only other potential clarinetist known to the police.

Clarkson lived in one of a street of small but pretentious houses, built as a successful speculation on the northern outskirts of Markhampton between the wars. He worked, with no great enthusiasm, as a sales manager in a local office. Trimble went to see him by appointment at six o'clock in the evening. Feeling the need for exercise, he walked from the police headquarters. Sergeant Tate accompanied him. The latter did not believe in unnecessary exercise, and his temper was not improved when the inspector beguiled the journey by cross-examining him on his recent activities.

"Have you finished looking into the matter of Ventry's bus on the night of the concert?" he asked.

"Yes, sir," said Tate stolidly. "You will have my report this evening. I hadn't quite time to finish typing it out," he added.

Trimble chose to disregard the allusion to his mania for typewritten reports.

You can tell me the result of your inquiry now," he said gra-
ly. "Let me see—it was bus routes 8 and 14 that you had to
look into, wasn't it?"

"Yes, sir. Ventry would normally take one of those two routes
from his house to the City Hall."

The sergeant seemed determined to be as uncommunicative as
possible, and Trimble had to prod him again.

"Well," he said. "What results did you get?"

"Very much what you anticipated, sir. We can eliminate the 14
bus, at any rate. There was only one which got to the City Center
at the time Ventry says he did, or within a quarter of an hour of it.
As it happens, the conductor knows him quite well by sight—he
owns a bull-terrier bitch and Ventry wanted to buy one of her
pups, I think he said—and he was quite positive he wasn't on his
bus that evening."

"Very good," the inspector said impatiently. "We can forget
about him—and the bull-terrier pups, too. What about the No. 8?"

"That isn't quite so satisfactory, sir. There are two busses to
consider there, being that they were running a relief that night,
three minutes after the regular one went down. The first conductor said he was certain he didn't stop anywhere that run between
the top of Telegraph Hill and the Worple Way corner—that's a
good half-mile past Ventry's house. He said he was full, outside
and in. I told him he ought to have stopped, full or not, at the fare
stage at the bottom of the hill, but that's what he says, anyway."

Tate paused to blow his nose. He seemed to Trimble to be
deliberately spinning out his story.

"The other conductor was one of those silly girls," he finally
went on. "I could tell as soon as look at her that she wouldn't be
able to notice anything. However, for what it was worth, I
showed her that snapshot of Ventry we got from the *Advertiser*
office, and she was ready to swear she'd never seen him, that
evening or any evening. But as I say, I don't think her observation
amounts to much. At best, I should call it a negative bit of evidence."

"You can call it negative if you like, Sergeant," said Trimble, "but it means that Ventry will never be able to prove his story about going down to the concert by bus. I was always sure he was lying."

"Yes, sir," said Tate in a noncommittal tone. He paused, and then added, "Of course, there's more than one way of lying."

"What exactly do you mean by that?" asked the inspector.

Tate seemed more reluctant than ever to explain himself. "Well, sir," he said at last. "I thought it might be worth while making inquiries, while I was about it, to see if he came by some other bus."

"Oh, you did, did you? I thought we were agreed that if Ventry took a bus from his house to the City Hall it must have been one of those two?"

"Yes, sir."

"Then why propose wasting time checking up on other busses?"

"Just in case he went to the concert from somewhere else than his own house, sir. That was what I meant by other ways of lying."

"Very well." Trimble made the concession grudgingly. "Find out what other busses reached the Center at about the right time, and have the conductors interviewed. It can't do any harm. Jeffrey can help you."

"I shan't want Jeffrey." Tate's placid voice hardened perceptibly for an instant. "As a matter of fact I finished the inquiry myself this morning. It's all in my report." And once more he became provokingly dumb.

Trimble would have given a good deal to be able to rejoin, "All right, I'll read it," and let the subject drop there and then, but it was beyond his powers, as Tate very well knew that it would be.

"Well?" he said, harshly. "I'm waiting. What was the result of your inquiry?"

"A No. 5A bus," said Tate in slow, deliberately flat tones, "reached the City Center at just six minutes past eight. According to the conductor, one of the passengers who alighted there exactly resembled the photograph of Ventry which I showed him."

"The man's mistaken, of course," said Trimble quickly. Extraordinary, he reflected even as he spoke, how calmly one could take a shock like that! Tate would never guess from his tone just what a disturbing blow the news had been. Thank God the sergeant hadn't that trick of guessing your thoughts that made the Chief so uncomfortable to deal with! "These identifications from photographs are unreliable things."

"Yes, sir." Tate was as noncommittal as ever. "The man seemed fairly confident about it, though."

"But he *must* be wrong!" Try as he would, a note of querulousness had crept into the inspector's voice. "A 5A bus! That route doesn't go anywhere near Ventry's house. It comes into the city from the north, doesn't it?"

"Yes, sir. Here's one of them coming towards us now."

A double-decked bus swung past them, tracing a golden glow through the gathering darkness.

"There you are!" Trimble gesticulated feebly after it. "How could Ventry, or anybody coming from his side of the town, have reached the City Hall in *that*?"

"Quite, sir. That's what I had in mind just now, when I said there was more ways of lying than one."

"Of course Ventry's lying! But it's sheer nonsense to suppose he should—" The inspector checked himself abruptly. He had allowed himself, against all his principles, to be betrayed into arguing the case with his subordinate. "I'd better see this conductor fellow myself, I suppose," he added, in the weary tone of the leader who had the distasteful task of clearing up his assistants' mistakes.

"Very good, sir," said the sergeant meekly.

They accomplished what was left of their journey in silence.

"Good evening, gentlemen!" Clarkson received the detectives with an eager smile. "Please forgive me if I kept you waiting at the door, but to tell you the truth I didn't think it could be you when I heard the ring. I was listening for the sound of a car. Never thought you would be walking. Well, well! Glad to think you're out to save the ratepayers' money! Just let me take your hats and coats and we'll go into the lounge. It's only in the pictures that detectives keep their hats on indoors, isn't it?"

Still chattering, he ushered the two men into a room, furnished in the height of the hire-purchase style of the mid-thirties. They were surprised to find that every item of the three-piece suite was already occupied. On the settee was a bald young man, fairly goggling with excited anticipation. One armchair was occupied by a plump, swarthy young woman who was simpering nervously behind her hand. In the remaining armchair another woman, fair-haired and good-looking, sat bolt upright with an expression of boredom and disgust on her hard, handsome features.

"This is the wife," said Clarkson, indicating the blonde. "And this is Tom and Maureen—friends of mine."

"Pleased to meet you," burst simultaneously from the lips of Tom and Maureen. The wife said nothing. It was apparent from the look that she gave her husband that she could have said a good deal.

Trimble bowed gravely in the general direction of the three-piece suite.

"I am delighted to make your acquaintance," he said. Turning to his host he went on smoothly. "Now Mr. Clarkson, I have one or two matters to discuss with you. Have you another room where the sergeant and I—"

"Oh, no!" Clarkson interrupted him. "That's not the idea at all! You see, Tom and Maureen are my alibis."

"Your *what?*" asked the inspector, genuinely startled.

"My alibis. So's the wife, only I don't know whether she counts in law—like witnessing a will, if you see what I mean. I say," he added anxiously, "I suppose it is the City Hall murder you've come up about, isn't it?"

"Yes," Trimble assured him, "it is." He caught Sergeant Tate's eye as he spoke, and for once in a way a gleam of mutual comprehension and amusement passed between them. "Perhaps you'd better tell us all about it," he added, and drew up a chair, leaving the sergeant to share the settee with Tom.

"Well, it's like this," Clarkson chattered on. "I take an interest in criminal matters, well, I suppose every intelligent person does more or less, but I take a particular interest as it so happens, and of course knowing as I do quite a lot of the fellows in the orchestra I was naturally very much interested indeed when I heard about the Mystery of the Missing Clarinet. (I don't know what you fellows call it, but that's the name I always think of it by. It seems to suit it somehow.) Well, it being pretty well an open secret that by all the rights I ought to have been the clarinet at that particular concert, and would have been if that chap Evans hadn't gone all stuck up and peculiar, when I heard that you were inquiring after me, I said to myself, 'Hullo, hullo! The Missing Clarinet is suspected to be Yours Truly!' Am I right?"

"Perfectly right," said Trimble emphatically.

"What did I tell you?" said Clarkson triumphantly to his wife, who looked, if anything, sourer than ever. "Well, I quite definitely wasn't the Missing Clarinet, and what's more I wasn't at the concert at all. If I'm not good enough to play, as I told Bill Ventry, then I'm damned if I'll pay good money to go and listen. That's what I thought, anyway. I'm not so keen on music as all that, though a chap must have a hobby of one sort or another. Of course, as it turned out, I simply cut off my nose to spite my face. When I found I'd missed a really front-page sensational murder, I was wild, I don't mind telling you. However, that's all over and done with and it's no good crying over spilt milk. But if you ask me"—here he leaned forward confidentially towards the inspector—"if you ask me, the chap to keep your eye on is that damned conceited prig, Clayton Evans. I wouldn't put it past him to bump a girl off just because she made a bloomer at rehearsal. He's simply crazy, that chap—crazy about music, that is. Of course, I'm fond of music myself, within reason—that's why I was so set on play-

142

ing in the orchestra, if he'd only let me have a decent part—"

"You were going to tell me about your alibi, Mr. Clarkson," Trimble reminded him gently.

"Sorry, old man, so I was. Afraid I do run on a bit. Look, won't you have a cigarette or something? I've been quite forgetting my manners.... Well, if you won't, I'll just light up myself, if you don't mind.... Well, as I was saying, the alibi. The long and the short of it is that instead of going to the concert we spent the evening with Tom and Maureen here."

"The whole evening?" asked Trimble solemnly.

"The whole evening. At least, I did. Wait a minute, I'll give you all the works. I know how particular you chaps are about trifles. Mind you, I don't mind—it's your job, I know. Anybody who's made a study of these things as I have can tell just how important trifles can be. Look. Tom and I work in the same office. We left together, about a quarter to six, and went straight to his place— that's in Charleville Road; only just round the corner. Maureen was there. Violet, that's the wife, didn't come along till quite a bit later. Where were you, by the way? We'd arranged to meet you there at six."

Mrs. Clarkson spoke for the first time since the detectives had entered the room.

"What the hell does that matter?" she said. "Get on with it, and don't waste the inspector's time."

"All right, all right," replied her husband, with an unexpectedly savage snarl. "It's not the first time you've been out on your own with no decent explanation, that's all. Anyway," he turned back to Trimble, "there it is. We had a few drinks until she did turn up, and then we had our evening meal—the four of us. After that we sat down to a quiet game of poker and it was eleven o'clock before we broke up. O.K.?" he appealed to Tom and Maureen.

"Absolutely," said Tom, who had been following this long and complicated narrative with breathless interest.

"Gospel truth," echoed Maureen.

143

"Thank you very much indeed," said Trimble. "You have made everything perfectly clear, Mr. Clarkson, and have been of the greatest assistance."

"That's all right, old man, that's all right. Only too glad to help. And now, if you won't think it rude of me, will you be wanting Tom and Maureen any more? Because if not, I think they rather want to get away—"

"Maureen's got something rather special in the oven," Tom explained.

Trimble, who felt that he had seen enough of the couple to last him a lifetime, assured them that their presence was no longer required in the interests of justice. Before they went he made them thoroughly happy by taking their names and address in his official notebook and adjuring them solemnly not to reveal what they had heard to anyone.

"There is one further matter, Mr. Clarkson," he said, when the alibis had taken their leave. "Is your clarinet in the house?"

"Yes, rather. I haven't touched it for months now. I've got it put away upstairs."

"You haven't lent it to anyone lately?"

"No."

"I wonder if I might have a look at it."

"Certainly, old man. I'll go and dig it out, I shan't be half a tick."

As soon as Clarkson was out of the room Trimble turned to Mrs. Clarkson. While he had been listening with half an ear to the long history of the alibi his mind had been busy on other things. The 5A bus that ran outside the Clarksons' door, some vague rumors which he had heard of Ventry's private life and the little incident of Mrs. Clarkson's late arrival at Tom and Maureen's, all suddenly came together in his brain and prompted him to take a leap in the dark.

"Tell me," he said quickly. "Did you see Mr. Ventry on the night of the concert?"

The response was immediate.

"What do you know about me and him?" she asked, biting her lips.

"Never mind. Answer my question. Did you see him?"

Mrs. Clarkson gave a swift glance towards the ceiling, where her husband's footsteps could be heard in the room above.

"No, I didn't, the swine," she muttered bitterly. "But I can tell you where he was. I tried to catch him at his house that evening, but he wasn't in. And all the time he was—"

She checked herself as the door opened and Clarkson appeared with a rather dusty black leather case.

"Here it is," he said. "Want to have a look at it?" He opened the case to reveal the instrument within, its parts carefully wrapped in cloth.

"Thank you," said Trimble. "You needn't bother to take it out. I just wanted to establish that it was there."

"I don't suppose I shall ever want to play it again," said Clarkson. "And to think that if I'd been willing to play second I might have been in on a murder! It just shows, doesn't it?"

"If you should want to sell it, I know of someone who has recently broken his own," the inspector observed. "Well, I won't keep you any longer, Mr. Clarkson. Good night!"

As he left the room he caught Mrs. Clarkson's eye. Behind her husband's back he held up his left hand and made the motions of writing on it with the other. She nodded to show that she understood.

"I think we might take a 5A bus home, Sergeant," observed Trimble when they got outside. He felt in a distinctly better humor than he had been when he entered the house. Although he was more uncertain than ever where the trail was leading him, he began to feel that it was leading somewhere. At all events, he had, in the last few minutes, unquestionably succeeded in impressing Tate, and that was a positive achievement.

15

Pettigrew Unbosoms Himself

"You'll have another whisky, Chief Constable," said Pettigrew. It was not a question, but a simple statement of fact. The Chief Constable would have another whisky and it would disappear as quickly, and with as little apparent effect on the consumer, as the two which had preceded it at dinner and the two more which would certainly follow it before the evening was over. This was Mr. MacWilliam's second visit to his house since they had met at the club, and he was beginning to wonder rather gloomily what he should do if the investigation into the Carless case outlasted his meager supplies of liquor.

"Thank you," said the Chief Constable. He helped himself liberally from the decanter, added the minimum of soda water and half emptied his glass at a gulp. "I've left a couple of bottles for you in the hall," he added.

"You've—*what?*" asked Pettigrew faintly.

"I have never been able to understand," said MacWilliam, looking meditatively at the glass in his hand, "why, in these days of shortages and rationing, it should be considered perfectly proper for guests to bring with them morsels of tea and sugar and disgusting little packets of margarine for the benefit of their hosts, while it is taken for granted that they should be supplied ad libitum with substances far more precious and—if you will forgive my mentioning it—a great deal more expensive. Now I don't very much care for tea and hardly take any sugar, but I do—as you may conceivably have observed—drink an appreciable quantity of whisky of an evening. I repeat, therefore, I have left two bottles for you in the hall."

Pettigrew opened his mouth to protest, but thought better of it. There was a finality about the Chief Constable's tone and a doggedness about the set of his jaw that put any argument on the subject out of the question.

"It is very kind of you," he ventured.

"Not at all. A simple matter of justice." The man seemed rather touchily anxious that no question of gratitude should enter into the matter.

Pettigrew tried another tack. "Well," he said, "if that is the case, I think I will have another glass myself."

The Chief Constable thawed at once. "That was what I had been waiting for you to say," he remarked genially. "Your very good health, sir!"

By common consent nothing had been said during dinner on the subject of his visit. MacWilliam had proved an agreeable guest, with a wide range of interests and a conversational gift that had met with Eleanor's instant approval. It was only now, when, coffee concluded, the two men had adjourned to the tiny cubbyhole which Pettigrew dignified by the title of study, that the business of the evening was due to begin.

Pettigrew seemed distinctly reluctant to begin it, none the less. He mixed his drink, lit cigarettes for himself and his guest, made an unnecessary to-do about finding ash trays and placing them in convenient positions, and was positively fussy over the arrangement of cushions in his armchair. When he finally sat down he remained silent and almost embarrassed, staring at the electric fire that warmed the little room.

"You must be regretting," said MacWilliam unexpectedly, "that it isn't a good old-fashioned grate."

"Eh?"

"Something to fiddle with," the Chief Constable explained. "Something to poke, or put coal on, or puff at with a pair of bellows or just curse for smoking. Something to occupy you, in fact, and help postpone the evil moment."

Pettigrew flushed guiltily, and then grinned. He found it impossible to be annoyed by this man, impertinent as he might be.

"I feel that I've brought you here on false pretenses," he said.

"I was under the impression that I had invited myself."

"Allowed you to come here on false pretenses, then."

"Maybe. Though I hardly think you'd have made such a pother if it was simply a question of telling me that you had nothing to say. In any case I have a few more reports that have come in during the last week which I want to leave with you. But we'll discuss them later. At the moment I want to listen to you."

"I don't know what you're expecting to hear," said Pettigrew, "but if it's a cut-and-dried explanation of how this murder was done and who by, you are not going to get it. You asked me to keep my eyes and ears open, I remember, and so I have done, but as neither my sight nor hearing are particularly keen, and I have no gift for extracting confidences, I haven't even any fresh bit of information to add to what you already have. Except one, now I come to think of it, and you can make what you can of it. Personally, I think it merely adds to the difficulties of the business. Here it is: Mrs. Basset is perfectly justified in saying that her watch is a reliable timekeeper. I ascertained that, unaided, by a superb piece of detective work the day before yesterday."

"Um!" said the Chief Constable, and helped himself to another drink.

"That is the beginning and the end of my factual contribution to the problem," Pettigrew proceeded. "Now for my general impressions about the case. I believe that this was a carefully calculated crime, committed for a valid and compelling motive. If I am right in that, then I can see only one individual who could have had such a motive or been capable of such calculation. At the same time, the facts your Inspector Trimble has so patiently collected make it quite impossible for that individual to have committed it. I trust I make myself quite clear?"

"Perfectly," said the Chief Constable with the utmost solemnity.

"On the other hand, if the murderer is any person other than the one who, as I say, could not possibly have killed Miss Carless, then we are faced with a perfectly staggering collection of coincidences instead of a logical sequence of events. The only solution that will fit—and I confess that I am far from happy about it—is to assume that this murder was the work of two hands—or, to be more accurate, of one brain and a wholly separate pair of hands, and highly specialized hands at that. Why the brain should have taken the appalling risk of employing an accomplice to do the dirty work, instead of using some other, safer method, I don't see. Still less do I understand what influence could have been brought to bear on the hands to compel them to do a horrible act from which they could derive no profit whatever. But there it is. Unless we premise the hands, the case against the brain falls to the ground."

"The hands being highly specialized," remarked the Chief Constable, "I take it that there are not many candidates for the position."

"Precisely. That ought to make it all the easier for you. But how you are going to make a case against the brain, short of a confession from the hands, is a bit of a problem."

"Suppose we leave that problem until it arises?" said MacWilliam. "At the moment what interests me is the identity of the person you call the brain."

Pettigrew said nothing for some moments. His gaze had reverted to the glowing orange bar of the fire, his hands were clasped, and his nose was wrinkled in an expression of discomfort and anxiety.

"I don't really *know* anything," he said at last. "That's what I meant when I talked about getting you here on false pretenses. It's just an impression, built upon—what shall I call it?—atmosphere, intuition—that, and an elementary point of law," he added. "There may be absolutely nothing in it, but a little simple research will at least demonstrate whether the thing is feasible or not. That is a police job—a simple matter of ferreting round Somerset House. I have an idea that the Surrogate might be helpful, too—if you can persuade him that it's his duty to talk."

"The Surrogate, eh?" The Chief Constable was looking at his host with an expression in which exasperation and amusement were nicely blended.

"I go on beating about the bush in this way," Pettigrew groaned, "simply because I can't bring myself to perform the good citizen's duty of peaching on his fellow human being. I can't be sure, you see. It's this business of an accomplice that bothers me—it seems to make such nonsense of the whole thing. It's clean out of character, and that alone throws a horrid doubt over the whole theory. And don't tell me that it's the function of the jury to decide," he added, with a sudden spurt of anger. "I've seen too many juries."

"A minute ago you said that we should have a job to make out a case against him."

"Did I? How filthily logical and consistent you are. I suppose policemen can't afford to indulge in any decent feelings. Look, I'll be honest with you, and myself. I'll simply tell you what I saw and heard, beginning from the beginning and going right through to the moment when the estimable Trimble appeared on the scene. I'll nothing extenuate nor ought set down in malice. Then if you come to the same conclusion that I do, in the light of all the knowledge you've acquired since, let the law take its course. My conscience will be clear. Like Pontius Pilate, I wash my hands. By the way, that reminds me—do you want to—?"

"Thanks," said MacWilliam. "Perhaps it would be as well."

150

"To begin with," said Pettigrew, when the discussion was resumed a little later, "do you read Dickens?"

"Yes. I suppose I've read all of him one time or another."

"*David Copperfield?*"

"That's the best of the lot, to my way of thinking."

"Cheers! Hold fast to *David Copperfield*. He's the nub of the case so far as I'm concerned. Now Lucy Carless, God rest her soul, didn't like Dickens. No, I'm wrong—and accuracy is all-important in these matters. She *hated* Dickens. And *David Copperfield*, she declared, was the worst of the lot. I know it takes a bit of believing, but I am being perfectly truthful, and what is more, she seemed to be quite sincere about it."

"Just a moment," the Chief Constable put in. "When did she tell you this?"

"I apologize," said Pettigrew. "I said I would begin at the beginning, and then I was in such a hurry to get to *David Copperfield* that I skipped the preliminaries. Well, as you presumably know already, Ventry gave a party the evening before the concert. My wife and I were invited and ..."

Pettigrew continued speaking for quite a considerable time. The Chief Constable heard him out to the end without interruption of any sort, his long legs extended in front of him, his gaze directed at the ceiling, whistling a soundless tune to himself. When the recital was finished he said, without moving from his position, "As you say, it is an elementary point of law. There was a paragraph about it in one of the papers a week or two ago."

"You see what I'm getting at, then?"

"Ye-e-es. I see what you're getting at all right. It takes a bit of working out, though. Let me see..." He ran over various points on his fingers. "It accounts for most of them," he conceded. "Not quite all, but most. As you remarked just now, if your theory's right, it's a routine matter to confirm the facts." He sighed. "I don't know how I'm to manage Trimble over this," he went on. "It would break his heart to have the case solved behind his back."

Pettigrew felt a sudden uneasy qualm in the pit of his stomach.

"Do you think the case is solved then?" he asked.

"Well, no, I don't," the Chief Constable rejoined with surprising cheerfulness. "We've got a long way to go yet, even supposing the facts match up to your very attractive supposition. There's hope for Trimble yet."

He appeared to become suddenly conscious of the empty glass at his elbow. Pettigrew took immediate steps to remedy the situation.

"And talking of facts," he went on, "I promised to let you see the further reports and statements I brought with me. I think you'll find them interesting."

He produced a small packet of typewritten papers. They brought the history of the investigation up to date, concluding with Trimble's report on his visit to the Clarksons' house. Pettigrew read them through, at first casually, and then with growing attention as he neared the end. When he reached the final page his face was blank with disappointment. He turned back and read over again some of the sheets, this time with anxious concentration.

"Why didn't you let me see these before?" he asked accusingly, when his scrutiny had come to an end.

"Well," said MacWilliam with a deprecatory air, "I could see that you had something on your mind, and I didn't want to distract you."

"Distract me be blowed! If you'd given me these when you first came in you'd have saved me from making a fool of myself! Surely you can see as well as I can that they knock the bottom out of my case?"

"I think you're exaggerating a little." The Chief Constable remained as calm as ever. "But I'd go so far as to say that these reports don't supply the bottom that your case needs if it's to hold water."

"'And it shall be called Bottom's Dream, because it hath no bottom,'" said Pettigrew bitterly. "Well, let's forget it! I have been

152

wasting your time, Chief Constable. It'll be a lesson to you not to ask for amateur help behind the backs of your detective force in the future." He laughed. "Funny to think that just now I was sweating blood because I didn't want to throw suspicion on somebody who—"

"And now you're relieved because you think you've been proved wrong," MacWilliam interrupted him. "Man, you're nothing but a bundle of inconsistencies! You've just produced the only logical, consistent explanation for the whole sequence of events, and now you want to drop it like a hot potato."

"I want to drop it because it leads straight to a plain, blank impossibility."

"If the logical solution is an impossibility, then either there is something faulty with the logic or the impossibility is a delusion," said the Chief Constable confidently. "Now I maintain that your logic is good, subject to verification of the facts on which your hypothesis is based. I propose to proceed with the verification, and if that works out as it should, then we will take a good look at the impossibility, and see what becomes of it. It is time I took myself off," he continued. "Good night to you, Mr. Pettigrew. It has been a most interesting evening. I'll be seeing you again later."

"I like your Chief Constable, Frank," said Eleanor when he had gone. "But do you suppose he is good at his job?"

"Very good, I should think."

"I shouldn't imagine that he had many original ideas of his own."

"Perhaps not, but he has a very ruthless way with other people's ideas."

Eleanor looked at her husband narrowly.

"You don't sound very happy about it," she observed.

"I'm not," he confessed. "I feel that I have started something, and I don't quite know where it will end. I have a horrible feeling that it may simply end in MacWilliam uncovering a very ugly

153

skeleton in somebody's cupboard, which will do nobody any good, and may do a lot of harm. If it doesn't end that way—"

"Well?"

"Then it will end in uncovering a corpse in the same cupboard, which will be more horrible still."

"Frank?"

"Yes?"

"Wouldn't you like to tell me about everything? I might be able to help you."

Pettigrew shook his head. "I want to keep you out of this, if I can," he said. "And I don't really think you could help. One thing you could do for me, perhaps—reach me down that book in the corner of the top shelf."

"Grove's *Dictionary of Music*, do you mean? Which volume do you want?"

"No, no, I mean Hobbes's *Leviathan*, next to Grove. There's something there that seems apt to my present state of mind."

He turned the pages until he found the passage that he sought. "Here it is," he said, and read aloud:

Sometime a man desires to know the event of an action; and then he thinketh of some like action past, and the events thereof one after another; supposing like events will follow like actions. As he that foresees what will become of a Criminal, re-cons what he has seen follow on the like Crime before; having this order of thoughts, the Crime, the Officer, the Prison, the Judge, and the Gallowes.

"The last word ought to be 'Home Secretary,' to bring it up to date," Eleanor said. "But it's a lovely passage, and it would be a pity to spoil it."

"You comfort me with your wise words," said Pettigrew, closing the book. "I shall go and put away Mr. MacWilliam's noble gift and then come to bed."

16

Select Dance

A thick envelope addressed in spidery handwriting was among Inspector Trimble's post next day. It was marked "Private and Confidential," heavily underscored.

INSPT. TRIMBLE [the letter began abruptly]: You asked me if I had seen a certain person on the day of somebody else's alibi and I told you I hadn't which was absolutely true, but I did know where he had been. It's absolutely no business of mine what he was up to, because I'm absolutely through with him and wouldn't touch him with a barge pole after he let me down like he did. He was always talking about being careful and of course he is a coward like that sort of men always are but actually it wasn't that at all but just that he'd found another woman. All I can say is I'm sorry for her and hope she doesn't go through what I have done. I had my suspicions when I saw them at his party the night before but now I know and that's why I don't mind telling you. He'd been putting me off and putting me off but I meant to have it out with him so that morning I phoned him and said I'd come round to his place about half-past five. He pretended to be ever so glad and said he'd run me down to M's before he went to the concert so I shouldn't be late and look suspicious. Well I got a 5A bus down to the center and there was a 14 just coming so I was there quite a bit before half-past five and he wasn't there. I rang and rang and no one answered and then I thought perhaps I was early though he said he would be coming straight home from the rehearsal so I hung about outside until nearly six and then I came away. I waited ages for a bus back to the center and when I got there I was so scared of being late I couldn't wait for a 5A and walked up. I took the short cut to Charleville Road through Fairfield Avenue. Well, you know how the houses on the N. side of the Avenue sort of lay back from the road with drives leading up to them. There was a car outside No. 6, not in the drive but close up to the fence in the road. I thought it was sort of peculiar to put a car there without any lights on or anything because of course it was getting dark and then I thought it looked sort of familiar so I went to look and it was *his* car. So if you want to know where he was that evening you can go and ask the lady at No. 6 and see what sort of answer you get. Only don't expect me to give any evidence about it because I'm not saying anything or signing anything. This is just an annonimous letter with no names mentioned because I think you ought to know.

P.S. You can see over into Fairfield Avenue from the back of Charleville Road so when I got to M's I went up to powder my nose in her bathroom and I took a peek out of the bathroom window and the car wasn't there any more, so I must have only just caught it. I thought you ought to know this.

Trimble passed the letter over to Sergeant Tate with an air of triumph. The latter read it through slowly and in silence.

"Six, Fairfield Avenue!" he said, taking off his ancient spectacles and carefully putting them away. "But that's Mr. Dixon's house!"

"Also Mrs. Dixon's," observed Trimble.

"This man Ventry," said the sergeant solemnly, "is no better than a satire, if you ask me."

Trimble made no comment.

"It's a pity the lady can't be a bit more precise about the time," Tate went on.

"Whatever the time was," said the inspector, "it seems pretty clear that he left Fairfield Avenue in plenty of time to get to Eastbury Junction to meet the train."

"That's what bothers me. I don't see how he could have, if he was on the bus."

"If he *was* on the bus."

"Well, the conductor seemed pretty sure of him."

"I told you, I shall want to have a talk to that conductor myself."

"Yes, sir, you did," said Sergeant Tate in an absolutely expressionless voice. "Will you be wanting to interview Mr. Schlumberger also?"

"Mr. Who?"

"Mr. Schlumberger—the other clarinetist who was engaged for the concert."

"Of course, I remember. We got his name and address from the list Mr. Dixon gave us. What about him?"

"There's a report just come through from the Yard," the sergeant said. "The Chief asked me to let you have it. I've got it here."

"Let me see it," said Trimble in the resigned voice of one who expects bad news.

The detective-sergeant who had been given the task of interviewing Mr. Schlumberger at his home at Herne Hill wasted no words.

"I interviewed the above-named man this morning, and showed him the copy photographs supplied," his report ran. "He studied them carefully and then made the written statement enclosed."

The enclosure was to this effect: "I am bad at remembering faces and I am not at all interested in strangers. I do not think I could recognize again the performer who sat next to me at this concert. The photographs produced do not seem to me to resemble the person in question. One of them reminds me rather of an old acquaintance of mine named Ventry, but it is not a very good likeness. HENRICH SCHLUMBERGER."

"No," said Trimble. "No. I do not think I shall want to see Mr. Schlumberger." He laid the report down. "Of course," he said hopefully, "he may have been disguised. He must have been disguised—whoever he was. The man is bad at remembering faces, too, and not interested in strangers."

"An old acquaintance of mine named Ventry," the sergeant murmured.

"Clarkson could have pinched that car easily enough," Trimble went on, frowning at the interruption. "That won't do, though. He was at Charleville Road when his wife arrived, and it had gone by then. All right! Let's suppose this Schlumberger person is correct and Ventry didn't take the clarinet's part. That doesn't mean he didn't drive to Didford and ditch the other fellow. It was too much of a risk for him to go on to the platform, so he got someone else...someone else ..."

His voice trailed away. His fingers drummed nervously on the table before him. For the first time he looked completely at a loss—and entirely human. Sergeant Tate, who was a good-natured man, to his astonishment found himself actually feeling sorry for the fellow. He coughed in an embarrassed fashion, cleared his throat and, seeking for words of comfort, finally said: "I dare say that bus conductor was mistaken. We'll see him again."

The gesture was not lost on the inspector. A grateful smile flitted for a moment across his face, but his despondency remained.

"Yes, we'll do that," he said. "But even if he is wrong, that won't take us much farther."

"And then we'll put it across Ventry good and proper," Tate went on. (It was strange how easily the "we" of the old City Police days came to his lips again, and how naturally the inspector seemed to take it.) "He's told too many lies. We could break him down easily now."

"No," said Trimble. "We don't want to go back to Ventry yet. Not until we're sure of our ground and can nail his lies to the counter. Before we tackle him I think a chat with Mrs. Dixon is indicated." He rose to his feet. "The bus conductor first," he said. "What's his name?"

"Barry."

"Get on to the bus depot and find out when Barry will be available. Then we'll tackle Mrs. Dixon. Then Ventry. Damn it, Tate, between the three of them we ought to be able to clear this case up somehow!"

There followed a day of maddening frustration. The omnibus company, after prolonged research, discovered that Barry was taking a week's holiday. They supplied his home address where he lived with his parents. Tate went to the address in a back street behind the cathedral and found an empty house. After patiently waiting for half an hour he encountered Mrs. Barry returning from shopping, and learned from her that her son was "off for the day," and that she did not expect to see him home till midnight. When pressed for his whereabouts she finally recollected that among his engagements was a Select Dance at the Masonic Hall that evening, where he was to act as Master of the Ceremonies. The sergeant had no better luck with Mrs. Dixon. She had gone to London for the day and would not be home before dinner.

Further work on the case was perforce postponed until the evening, and the rest of the day was occupied in clearing off accumulated arrears of routine work. At a little before nine the two detectives left the police headquarters together.

An extremely elegant young man with a superb handle-bar mustache was just announcing a Paul Jones as they pushed through the doors of the Masonic Hall. They advanced up the room through an inferno of noise, avoiding with difficulty the whirling circle which filled the dancing floor. The Master of the Ceremonies bore down upon them at once.

"This is a select dance, you know, chaps!" he said in a voice that somehow made itself heard above the din of the band and the stamping of feet. "Admission by ticket only."

"We haven't come here to dance!" Trimble shouted back.

At that moment the music mercifully switched to the comparatively soothing strains of a slow fox trot, and the two revolving circles of men and women split into couples. The young man looked blankly at Trimble and then at Tate.

159

"Good Lord, it's the detective-type again!" he said. "What have I been up to now?"

"The inspector would like a word with you, Mr. Barry," the sergeant explained.

Mr. Barry nodded briefly, and strode up to the platform at the end of the hall.

"Keep the Paul Jones going till I get back, Sammy," he said to the band leader. "Shan't be a minute." Then he beckoned the detectives to follow him and led the way out of the hall. A corridor ran parallel with the side of the dance floor and here the three men established themselves in wickerwork armchairs. "We're lucky," Barry went on. "We've got the place to ourselves. A little later and it would be full of canoodling couples. By the way, you heard what I said to the band just now? Well, seven minutes is the extreme limit for a Paul Jones. Don't ask me why, but it is. If it goes beyond that, there'll be a riot. So make it snappy, won't you?"

Trimble took the hint and wasted no time on preliminaries. "You made a statement to the sergeant here yesterday," he said. "Just look through this copy to refresh your memory."

Barry took the sheet of paper given him and glanced over it rapidly. "That seems right enough," he said.

"Now look at this photograph again and tell me if you are sure—*sure*, mind, that it's the same man."

Barry studied the photograph and then turned a gaze of innocent inquiry on the inspector.

"Look, chaps," he said. "Which is it you want me to say—he is or he isn't? I've had to give evidence at a court martial in my R.A.F. days, and I know the way these lawyers can jigger you about. But if you tell me what's wanted I can stick to it, either way. Only I must have the dope first. What's it to be?"

"I want your honest opinion," said the inspector.

"That's a bit tough," said Barry with a frown. "If I ever find myself giving my honest opinion in the witness box I shall be made to look an ass as sure as fate. I tell you, I've seen it done.

160

Well, here goes!" He closed his eyes, as if plunging on some desperate gamble. "I'm pretty certain that was the blighter," he said at last. "I wouldn't mind having a friendly bet on it. But as to being dead sure—well, that's another matter."

Trimble persisted a little longer, but could get no more definite opinion from him, and presently the young man, glancing at his wrist watch, announced that the seven minutes allotted for the Paul Jones was nearly up.

"The fellows will be wanting to get back to their regular girls," he explained. "A Paul Jones is all very well for livening things up at the start, but they didn't pay for their tickets to see their girls dancing with other fellows. It's time I called it off and announced a rumba."

He moved off towards the dance hall. "You can get out that way," he said, pointing down the corridor in which they had been sitting.

Sergeant Tate was about to move off in that direction, but the inspector restrained him. "I think we'll come back to the hall for a moment," he said.

"Just as you like, chaps," the M.C. replied. "You won't have much chance of partners, now the Paul Jones is over, but I'll see if I can fix you up, if you like."

Trimble declined the offer with thanks on his own behalf and Tate's. The two officers followed Barry back into the hall. Just inside the door the inspector drew Tate into a corner, and looking towards the platform said, "Sergeant, do you see what I see up there?"

Tate looked in the same direction, and scrutinized each of the players in turn.

"Good Lord!" he said. "Isn't that Whatsisname playing the thingmebob?"

"Zbartorowski playing the clarinet," Trimble corrected him. "I spotted him as we came in."

"Funny, that," the sergeant said ruminatively. "He must have got hold of another one. He'd never have had time to get the old one mended. Would it be worth while having a word with him, do you think, sir?"

Trimble nodded in agreement.

With a look of resignation in his sorrowful brown eyes, Zbartorowski came from his place in the band at the inspector's summons.

"So you're playing again, I see," said Trimble.

"If you can call this playing—yes," the Pole replied with a shrug of his shoulders.

"Did you have your instrument repaired, then?"

"No." Zbartorowski shuddered at what was obviously a painful memory. "No. I have now another."

"Where did you get it from?"

"Mister—the fat man who plays the organ—"

"Ventry, do you mean?" the inspector put in sharply.

"That is the name—Ventry. He lend it to me till I can buy a new one."

Trimble drew a deep breath. "The devil he did!" he murmured.

Zbartorowski looked more troubled than ever. "I was wrong to take it?" he said anxiously. "It is stolen, perhaps? I promise you, sir, I did not know—"

"No, no," Trimble hastened to comfort him. "You've done nothing wrong—so far as I know. Only it happens that this particular instrument—"

"Just a minute, sir," Tate put in. "It occurs to me, Ventry told us he had three of these things, all different. They had letters, I remember. The missing one was a B something or other."

"B flat—yes," Zbartorowski said. "That is the one I have here. These dance band parts, they are scored for the B flat. But it is not missing. Mr. Ventry lend it me and I did not think it was wrong to take it."

"What I want to know," said the inspector, "is how he came to let you have it. You don't know him well, do you? You couldn't even remember his name just now."

"It is quite simple," Zbartorowski explained. "Mr. and Mrs.

162

Dixon came to dinner with Mrs. Roberts and I am in the kitchen to wash up. You know, Mrs. Roberts is always very kind to me and so she ask Mr. Dixon to come and speak to me because he can talk my language, and Mr. Dixon ask me what I am doing now and if I will play at the next concert, and I told him I can no more play because of—of what you know, and Mr. Dixon he say, 'In that case I will find you a good clarinet because I know a man who has one he do not require,' and so this morning he telephone me and say Mr. Ventry will give it me if I go to his house and I go there and he give it me. But it is a loan only, until the next orchestre concert—if Mr. Evans will let me play," he concluded.

"And that appears to be that," remarked Trimble as they left the dance hall. "We will get Dixon to verify that Polish fellow's story, but it seems genuine enough. If it is, here's one more poser for Master Ventry to answer. If his clarinet was missing on the night of the concert, how did he come to have it this morning?"

"He seemed surprised enough to find it gone when we were at his house," Tate remarked.

"Then, at the least, it can only mean that he has since recovered it somehow and not said a word to us about it, which is suspicious in itself. First cars, and then clarinets," said Trimble, with an unwonted touch of humor. "He's a master at losing things and finding them again. Has it occurred to you," he added, "that if anybody wanted to make it quite impossible to prove who played that instrument on the night of the concert he could hardly do better than do just what Ventry has done?"

Tate was not yet accustomed to the new relationship of confidence that had sprung up between himself and his superior. Surprise at being asked for his opinion made him a little slow in the uptake.

"Oh, ah, I see! Fingerprints!" he said at last.

"Exactly, fingerprints. Obviously, if that was the clarinet played at the concert it would be smothered with the prints of the player. If anyone wants to get rid of them, he can do one of two things— either wipe it clean, which will look suspicious when it comes to be examined, or, better still from his point of view, give it to somebody else to play on. One Paul Jones, and every print is obliterated by Zbartorowski's. The instrument's quite useless for our purposes now—that's why I didn't bother to take it away from him this evening.

"Let's see how it works out," he went on, as the pair trudged away from the Masonic Hall through the quiet streets of Markhampton. "Ventry 'misses' his clarinet on the night of the concert; in other words, he lends it to—X, let's call him, to take Jenkinson's place at the concert. Ventry himself, of course, does the job of meeting Jenkinson at the station and dumping him. Whether Ventry or X actually commits the murder I can't make out at the moment. After it is done X returns the clarinet to Ventry, and he takes this means of making it useless for purposes of identification. Oh, I know," he went on hurriedly as the sergeant drew breath to speak. "We haven't a ghost of an idea who X is, and we don't yet know of any motive Ventry could have for killing Miss Carless, and that damned man Barry would make a superb witness for the defense. Don't tell me, sergeant, I know, I know!"

"I was only going to say, sir," said Tate soberly, "that it seems to have been Mr. Dixon who was responsible for the idea of lending the clarinet to Zbartorowski."

"Therefore, I suppose you would go on to say, Dixon must be X! When the one certain thing about this whole damned case is that he can't play a note on any instrument!"

"I quite realize that, sir. I only mentioned it because it seemed a little odd. I had been turning over in my mind whether it might possibly be a case of Dixon and X, or Dixon and Ventry and X, or ..."

The possibilities of the case stretched before them indefinitely, as endless and uninviting as the steep slope of Fairfield Avenue, which they were just then ascending.

17

The Truth About Ventry

The Dixons were proud in the possession of a resident maid—a stiff-jointed, sour-faced creature with unaccommodating manners, but a resident maid none the less. It was she who opened the door to the detectives, admitted that Mrs. Dixon was in, and showed them into what was evidently Dixon's study, ordering them, rather than asking them, to wait. Within a minute or less the door opened and Dixon himself came into the room.

"You wished to see me, I understand?" he said.

"I am afraid your servant must have made a mistake," replied Trimble. "Actually, it was Mrs. Dixon we asked for."

"My wife? I don't understand. What conceivable interest can you have in my wife?"

"I should prefer to explain that to her personally."

Dixon and Trimble were much of a size. They faced each other across the little room with wary, appraising eyes, like two lightweight boxers just entering the ring. Dixon was pale, his chin thrust out aggressively, his hands buried in his coat pockets. It was obvious that he was prepared to take offense at the least provocation, and equally obvious from which direction he looked for the offense.

"You will not explain anything to my wife," he said sharply, "except in my presence."

It was the third time that Dixon had used the expression "my wife," Trimble noticed. Each time it had been spoken with an unmistakable emphasis that had grown sharper at every repetition. Obviously a possessive type of husband, he thought. Possessive—and nervous. It was not a very happy combination of qualities, considering the nature of the inquiry on which he was now engaged. He had the disagreeable feeling that what he was about to do that evening might well result in personal disaster to two quite innocent people, without really advancing the investigation an inch. But it had to be done. He had chosen to become a detective, and it was too late in the day to complain that the trade was sometimes incompatible with gentlemanly behavior.

"Of course, Mr. Dixon," he said, "you are entitled to be present when Mrs. Dixon is interviewed, if you so desire. It is entirely a matter for you—and for her."

"My wife's wishes will be the same as mine in this respect," said Dixon sharply and rather jerkily. "I repeat, I cannot imagine what possible interest you should have in seeing her—but I suppose that you are still concerned with the death of Mrs. Sefton— as you were on the last occasion that I saw you—when I gave you all the help I could—as I always shall."

"The matter arises out of that case—yes, sir. We believe that Mrs. Dixon may be in a position to help us."

Dixon shrugged his shoulders, and was apparently about to make some angry retort. He evidently thought better of it, however, for he spun round on his heel, and muttering, "Very well, I'll fetch her," made for the door.

Before he could leave the room the inspector, prompted by Sergeant Tate, spoke again.

"One moment, sir," he said. "You said just now that you were ready to assist us. Well, there is one small matter on which I should like your help, and as it does not affect Mrs. Dixon in any way perhaps we could deal with it straightaway."

"By all means. What is it?" It was noteworthy that now the matter concerned himself, and not his wife, Dixon was perfectly at ease.

"We have just been interviewing a man named Zbartorowski. I think you know him."

"Mrs. Roberts foisted him on to the orchestra and I vetted him on Evans's behalf. That is the extent of my knowledge of him. Why?"

"He tells us that you procured the loan of a clarinet for him from Mr. Ventry. Is that so?"

"Perfectly correct. He had broken his instrument in a fit of drunkenness and asked me where he could find another. I knew Ventry had one which he did not use, and promised to mention the matter to him. Why not?"

"Were you aware that Mr. Ventry's clarinet was missing on the night of the concert?"

"Obviously I should not have asked Ventry to lend an instrument if I had thought it was missing. Is that all?"

"That is all, sir, thank you."

Dixon went out and returned almost immediately with Nicola.

"My wife has had a long and tiring day," he announced. "I must therefore ask you to be as brief as possible."

He led her to the one comfortable armchair which the room contained, settled her in it, and remained standing behind its back, as though to protect her from assault.

Whether because she was tired or not, Nicola Dixon was paler than usual. Her head drooped, so that as she sat in the low chair there was little that the detectives could see of her except a mass of auburn hair.

"Mrs. Dixon," Trimble began, "my colleague and I, as you are aware, are inquiring into the death of Lucy Carless on the occasion of the recent concert at the City Hall. For that purpose we are anxious to check, as far as possible, the movements of various individuals on that evening."

"My wife," put in Dixon from behind the chair, "was at home

the whole of that evening up to the time of the concert itself."

"Excuse me, sir," said the inspector firmly. "I raised no objection to your being present at this interview, but I must ask you not to interfere. I require Mrs. Dixon's answers to my questions, and not yours."

Nicola raised her head for a moment.

"What does it matter?" she said in her rich, languorous tones. "It's perfectly true. I was in the whole afternoon and evening, right down to the time I left to go to the concert—and I only got there in time by the skin of my teeth. Mr. Pettigrew will tell you about that—he sat next me in the Hall. You can ask the man who helped me park my car, too, if you like. I expect he'll remember it, because I gave him half a crown. Hadn't got anything smaller," she explained.

"Make and number of the car?" Sergeant Tate asked automatically.

"It's a Collingwood Twelve. I haven't the least idea of the number—I've no head for figures."

"ZQM 592," Dixon interposed.

"Thank you."

"The point on which I particularly require your assistance, Mrs. Dixon," the inspector pursued, "is this: During the afternoon and evening, when, as you say, you were in, was anybody else with you in the house?"

Dixon drew in his breath with an audible hiss, and his hands gripped the back of the chair until the skin whitened round the knuckles, but Nicola herself showed no sign of emotion.

"No, I don't think so," she said in the same lazy, low-pitched voice. "It was the maid's day out, I know that, because I had to get tea for myself."

"You are quite sure, Mrs. Dixon?" The inspector's eyes for a moment strayed towards Dixon's mask-like face behind the chair, and his heart smote him. But duty was duty, and he steeled himself to go on. "I must ask you to be careful about this, because we have reason to believe otherwise."

Still Dixon said nothing. He was breathing hard, and staring down at the back of Nicola's head as though fascinated.

"I don't quite know what you mean." Her voice was as deliberate as ever, but not quite so level in tone.

"A car which was not yours was seen outside this house between the hours of six and seven on the evening in question. I have reason to believe that it belonged to one of the persons whose movements I am endeavoring to trace. It was a Hancock car and the number was—"

"Ventry, by God!" The words came from Dixon's lips with the force of an explosion. At the sound Nicola turned in her chair and looked up into his face. The detectives were unable to see her expression, but his was a study in concentrated fury.

"Mr. Dixon!" Trimble implored him. "I asked you just now—"

"Be quiet, you fool!" was the contemptuous reply. "I can handle this. How long was he here?" he demanded of the woman, crouched in an appealing attitude, her face within a few inches of his own. "He left the rehearsal early—he never turned up to play at the concert. What were you doing here all that time, the pair of you?"

Nicola made no reply. Slowly she drew away from the distorted angry countenance confronting her. Then she stood up and deliberately turned to face the inspector.

"What do you want to know?" she said, with a faint but purposeful stress on the word "you."

"I want to know particularly what time Mr. Ventry left this house."

Nicola was looking at the floor, her foot tracing patterns on the carpet. "I don't know exactly," she muttered. "My clock was all to hell—about twenty minutes wrong—that was what made me late at the concert—"

"Your bedroom clock, you slut!" came the furious comment from behind her. Nicola made no reply. She did not even turn her head, but remained standing, beautiful and forlorn, in the middle of the room.

Trimble steeled himself to go on.

"If you only left just in time to get to the concert before it began," he said, "it should be fairly easy to calculate when that was. Did Mr. Ventry leave at the same time?"

"No—he didn't leave with me—of course not—he had his own car," she faltered.

"But did you leave the house together?"

"Yes—no—I can't remember—I—"

"It is important that you should remember, Mrs. Dixon."

Nicola gulped twice and then said faintly, "He left first, I remember that."

"How long before you did?"

"Some time before, I don't know exactly. I—" As she spoke her legs appeared to give way beneath her and she would have fallen if Dixon had not come forward and caught her. By the time that he had helped her back to her chair she was in a state of collapse. Deliberately he turned his back on her and faced the inspector.

"My wife is in a delicate state of health," he said in the hard voice of a man under intense strain. "I do not propose to allow her to answer any further questions. I may have some of my own to put to her later, but that is my affair. Please be good enough to leave us now."

It was when the two detectives had nearly reached police headquarters that Sergeant Tate uttered his first comment on the scene which they had just witnessed.

"I never knew there was so many jealous husbands about," he said. "Do you realize, sir, that makes the third we've had to deal with in this case alone? Sefton, Clarkson, and now Mr. Dixon. It's really surprising, when you come to think of it. Of course," he added reflectively, "in a way it's a compliment to the ladies, I suppose."

"If I were to say what I think of Mrs. Dixon it would be anything but a compliment," said Trimble austerely.

*　　*　　*

When the inspector entered his office next morning he was greeted by an unexpected piece of news.

"Mr. Ventry has just been on the telephone asking for you," the sergeant on duty told him.

"What did he say?"

"He just wanted to know if it would be convenient for him to call and see you at half-past ten about the Carless case, sir. I told him that it would."

"You were quite right," said Trimble, and sat down to digest this new development. It was the first time, he reflected, since the case began, that anybody had offered to come forward and assist the police. It was somewhat ironical that the person to do so should be the very man who was next on his list for questioning, and some very awkward questioning, too. It was all to the good, inasmuch as it would save him a journey out to the other end of the town and he felt that he would be in a better position to extract the truth from this elusive customer on his own ground, in the clean air of police headquarters, than in the cigar-laden atmosphere of Ventry's music room.

But Ventry had a way of bringing his own atmosphere with him, and the scent of a rich Havana preceded him up the narrow stairs that led to Trimble's office. The inspector sniffed in disgust and Sergeant Tate, who did not share his superior's dislike of tobacco, in envy, as the patrician aroma reached their nostrils.

"Morning, Inspector," said Ventry, when he appeared, panting slightly. "Your stairs are bloody steep for a man in my condition. I know—don't tell me—smoking's bad for the wind, but you can't have everything. Look, I won't keep you long, but I thought you ought to see this. I should have given it you sooner, but I had to go to London yesterday, and I thought it would keep."

"This" proved to be a cardboard box, about eighteen inches long, six inches wide and as many deep, empty save for paper packing; a sheet of brown paper addressed to Ventry and bearing ten pennyworth of canceled stamps; and a length of stout string.

"It came by the afternoon post the day before yesterday," Ventry explained. "No letter or anything with it. And inside was—"

"Your B flat clarinet," Trimble could not resist interrupting.

"That was a jolly good guess," said Ventry in naïve admiration. "Anyhow, I thought this might be a help to you if you wanted to trace the chap who took it, so I—"

"It might have been even more help if you had brought us the clarinet as well as the packing, Mr. Ventry, instead of getting rid of it again immediately."

"Getting rid of it? I haven't. You can have the thing today if you really want to see it."

Trimble began to lose patience.

"I have already seen your instrument," he said. "It was then in the hands of another person to whom you had chosen to lend it, and for that reason was quite useless to me."

"Lord! You fellows know everything! How the devil did you get on to that? I only gave it to the man yesterday."

"That is neither here nor there, Mr. Ventry. Please let us stick to the point. A man of your intelligence must have understood that as soon as you realized what the parcel contained the proper thing to do was to take it to the police in exactly the condition in which it reached you."

Ventry nodded his head sagely, took his cigar from his mouth and knocked a generous supply of ash on to the floor.

"I know," he said, with the air of a proud schoolboy giving the correct answer. "Fingerprints."

"Well? And what is your explanation?"

"I'm afraid I made a bit of an ass of myself over that," said Ventry with unabashed geniality. "You see, it was just the fingerprint question that worried me. I knew if I brought you the thing down you'd find it simply stuck all over with fingerprints and all of them mine. And as one way and another I seem to be in a bit of a spot over this business, I just couldn't face it. You see, what happened was this—I opened the parcel, just as you might open any other parcel, thinking of nothing in particular, and as soon as I got

172

down among the paper stuff inside there was the old B flat. Well, you may think me a fool, but I'm a collector. I collect musical instruments and I *like* musical instruments, just as some people do watches or clocks or china dogs, so naturally the first thing I did was to fish it out and stick it together and go over it thoroughly, to make sure it wasn't damaged in any way. Of course, I know as well as you do that the proper thing to do was to pick it up with a pair of tongs and bring it down here to be tested or dusted or whatever the chaps do in books, but my mind simply wasn't working that way. I wasn't thinking of it as Exhibit A at somebody's trial, but as a damned good piece of craftsmanship which might have got knocked about after traveling through the post in a flimsy box like that."

He looked regretfully at the diminished stub of his cigar and threw it into the empty fireplace.

"Well," he continued, "it looked all right. There were one or two scratches on the polish of the wood, but none of the keys were damaged so far as I could see. But after all, there's only one way to tell if an instrument is in good order, and that is to see if it sounds right. There was a clean reed fitted to the mouthpiece—there's a clue for you, if you like—a perfectly good, clean reed—so I tried it over. It must be years since I played a clarinet, and I made some horrid squeaks at first, but it's astonishing how quickly a thing like that comes back, and in next to no time I was playing a silly little Vivaldi Gigue my father used to make me do every day by way of fingering practice. Sheer force of habit, I give you my word! As soon as I'd finished I realized what an ass I'd been, and I went all hot and cold when I thought of those damned fingerprints. I decided to put it away and sleep on it. When next day Dixon rang me up and asked me if I had an instrument to lend to that Polish blighter it seemed to me an easy way out. He could put his prints on top of mine, I thought. Sorry if I've destroyed a valuable clue and all that, but at least I had the sense to keep the paper and string."

Whatever Trimble's opinion of the story, he kept it to himself.

Instead, he picked up the sheet of brown paper and examined it closely.

"This doesn't look as if it would be particularly helpful," he remarked.

"No, it doesn't," Ventry agreed. "Block letters for the address, very thick writing. Looks to me as if it had been done with a matchstick dipped in ink instead of a pen. Postmark, Markhampton Central. The box is homemade, I should say. It might have been cut down from—"

"All these things will be examined in due course," said the inspector curtly, putting the bundle of paper and cardboard to one side.

"Sorry I butted in. Not my business, I know. Well, there it is." He rose. "Anything I can do to help you fellows—"

"Yes, there is. Please sit down again, Mr. Ventry. I have another question altogether to ask you. How did you go to the City Hall on the night of the concert?"

"Oh, but I've told you that one already. By bus."

"Which bus?"

Ventry stared at the inspector for a moment without speaking, and then a slow grin spread across his face.

"Oh, Lord!" he said. "Has somebody been talking?"

"I asked you, sir, which bus?"

"This is where my reputation goes below zero," said Ventry in a resigned voice. "It was a 5A."

Sergeant Tate, sitting in his corner, could not suppress a gasp of satisfaction.

"A 5A," Ventry repeated, turning towards him. "And more by token, the conductor had one of those wild Battle of Britain mustaches. I'd know him again anywhere. I only hope he'd know me. I'm afraid you'll want to have anything I say checked up, after all the trouble I've given you," he explained.

"Then you did not go to the concert direct from your house?"

"I did not. I never went near my house from the time I left

174

the rehearsal till the concert came to its sticky end."

"Your car was stolen—"

"Oh, my car was stolen all right. That was the trouble."

"Your car was stolen," the inspector repeated, "not from your house but from outside No. 6 Fairfield Avenue."

"It was. You've got the whole thing taped, Inspector, and I've been lying like a trooper about it—all for the love of a lady. Who says the age of chivalry is dead?"

"I think, Mr. Ventry," said Trimble coldly, "that it is about time we heard the truth from you."

"Right-oh!" said Ventry cheerfully. "Though I think you've found out pretty nearly all of it off your own bat. You see, I've been making passes at Nicola Dixon for quite a time now, and just lately she's been responding more than a little. From something I overheard at the rehearsal I knew that the coast would be clear the rest of the evening so far as that codfish of a husband of hers was concerned, so I decided to try my luck. I rang her up, and she was in. I drove up to her house, and everything went according to plan. We had a few drinks, we had a bite of supper, we had some fun and games, and then, a bit late in the day, we found out that her clock was twenty minutes slow."

"Her bedroom clock?"

"Saving your presence, it was her bedroom clock. That was a bit of a shock, knowing what a stickler Evans is for starting his shows on the dot, but there was just time still, and I was pretty sure I could make it comfortably in the car. The real shock came later. Nicola's car was in the drive and she got in first. Mine was in the road, tucked away against the hedge so as not to be too conspicuous. At least, that's where it had been. When I got there, it wasn't. I shouted to stop Nicola—she was only just out of the drive—but she was in low gear and couldn't have heard me. So there I was, planted. And the rest of my story," he concluded with simple pride, "is perfectly true."

"Thank you," said Trimble. He sat silent for a moment and

then went on, "I won't ask you, sir, why you have chosen to conceal the truth until now, because the reason is as obvious as it is disreputable."

"I am a damned disreputable fellow," Ventry agreed cheerfully. "By the way, does Dixon know about this?"

"He does, sir. You will have to face the consequences of that."

"Oh, consequences! One thing I can be sure of. He'll never divorce Nicola on my account!"

With this enigmatic observation the interview terminated.

18

The Truth About K.504

"There are two steps down," said the Chief Constable. "And mind your head."

He spoke just too late. Pettigrew negotiated the steps fairly successfully, but the low beam caught him sharply on the top of his skull. When he recovered he found himself in a small, square, paneled room, half filled by an enormous desk. It was the first time that he had ever penetrated into Mr. MacWilliam's tiny, medieval house, squeezed between two Palladian residences in a corner of Markhampton Cathedral Close.

The Chief Constable was busy with a corner cupboard behind the desk.

"With the Dean on one side of me and the Chancellor of the Diocese on the other, I live in what might be called a desirable neighborhood," he observed, emerging from the cupboard with a decanter, a siphon and two glasses. "None the less, I make it a point of honor not to invite anybody to this house over five feet six in height, if it can be avoided. The ancestors of the English must have been a squat race."

Pettigrew took the glass extended to him.

"I am sorry I couldn't invite you to my place," he said. "But my wife had asked some friends in to play bridge, and I thought you would prefer not to risk meeting them. Mrs. Basset was one of them," he added.

MacWilliam opened a bulky portfolio and took from it a mass of papers which he arranged upon the desk. Their appearance was depressingly familiar to his visitor. Then he opened a long envelope and added its contents to the pile.

"I agree," he said. "Your wife's guests were better avoided on this occasion, particularly Mrs. Basset. However, we should not be disturbed here this evening. I have given orders that I am not to be sent for except in an emergency. And I do not think there is much risk of one of my ecclesiastical neighbors dropping in." He leaned back in his chair and fixed Pettigrew with his candid open-eyed stare. "Talking of ecclesiastics," he went on, "you were perfectly right about the Surrogate."

"Oh," said Pettigrew.

"In fact, you were perfectly right all along."

"Oh," said Pettigrew again.

"Perhaps you would like to look at the papers to satisfy yourself that they are all in order."

"I suppose I might as well," said Pettigrew unenthusiastically. When he had glanced through them he said: "Yes, they seem to be quite conclusive. They certainly bear out my suggestions as to what happened."

"I congratulate you."

"Thanks." Pettigrew's tone was one of the deepest despondency.

"On the other hand," the Chief Constable went on in level tones, "the latest reports from Trimble don't seem to carry the matter very much farther."

Pettigrew, rapidly running through the reports, agreed that they did not. "In fact," he said, "we are exactly where we were when we started."

"Now there," said MacWilliam placidly, "I am unable to agree with you. We have done a great deal. We have established the truth of what seemed at first—you will forgive me for saying so— a wild and highly improbable theory. In so doing we have proved a number of highly suggestive facts. And the facts seem to me to point to one inescapable conclusion—namely, that we have identified at least one of the persons responsible for this crime. I think that is quite a lot to go on with."

"And where, my good Chief Constable," cried Pettigrew, losing his patience, "where do you go on from here? What is the good of all your suggestive facts and your inescapable conclusions when you know perfectly well that at the end of it all you can't say who committed the murder or how it was done? You say that I have been right all along, and so I have. But please to remember that this is exactly the situation which I foretold would arise when you dragged all this stuff out of me. Here we are with a mass of facts which may or may not concern the crime. We have no means of proving whether they do or don't. So we are left with the prospect of living here for the rest of our lives with a fellow citizen whom we suspect of having committed a murder, although the suspicion may be quite baseless. I wish to God I had obeyed my instincts and kept out of this business altogether!"

The Chief Constable's only reply to this tirade was to pick up the decanter and pour a generous helping into Pettigrew's glass, adding a minute quantity of soda water. Pettigrew gratefully accepted the peace offering and the two men sat in silence for a moment. Then, as MacWilliam was about to speak, the quiet was broken by the ringing of the front door bell.

MacWilliam rose quietly, drew the window curtain aside and peered out.

"This is rather awkward," he murmured, returning to the middle of the room. "Inspector Trimble is outside. It must be something important, or he wouldn't have come here in view of my instructions. My servant is out, so I shall have to let him in myself." He looked round the room in mock despair. "I ought to

179

have devised a bolthole from this place," he went on. "There's nowhere in it where a rat could hide. Perhaps, though, I could see him in the hall, and you stay here till he's gone."

"No, no," said Pettigrew resignedly. "Let him come in, by all means. It will make the perfect end to a delightful day."

MacWilliam still hesitated.

"It's the man's feelings I'm thinking about," he said.

"Damn the man's feelings! I don't see why I should be the only one to suffer over this diabolical affair."

The ring at the door was repeated, and the Chief Constable, with a shrug of his shoulders, went out of the room. Pettigrew heard the front door being opened and the sound of Trimble's voice in the hall.

"You will forgive my troubling you, sir, but it is a matter of such importance—" he was saying as he expertly negotiated the two steps down and with the ease born of long practice ducked his head at the right moment. He stopped short at the sight of Pettigrew. "I beg your pardon, sir," he said stiffly. "I was not aware you had a visitor. Perhaps you would prefer me to—"

At this point the inspector's eyes fell on the damning evidence laid out on the desk. It was a painful moment. A deep flush spread across his face as his superior's iniquity slowly dawned upon him. "I was not aware," he repeated, "—not aware, sir, that you—that Mr. Pettigrew…"

With something approaching horror Pettigrew perceived that there were actually tears in the man's eyes. His heart smote him, and he vainly sought for words of consolation, but no words came. One can apologize for most things, he reflected, but injury to a fellow man's professional pride is an offense almost beyond expiation.

The Chief Constable had his own remedy for this, as for almost every other, emergency. He reached quickly into the corner cupboard, found another glass, filled it and pressed it into Trimble's hand.

"Thank you, sir, but I do not drink," said the inspector coldly.

"I am aware of that, but on this occasion you do. You're in need of a dram. Drink it up, and sit down—or better, sit down first."

He pushed a chair behind Trimble, just in time. The inspector sat down so abruptly that the contents of the glass were in danger of being spilled. He seemed to be in a daze, and automatically carried the glass to his lips and took a long drink. The strength of the spirit caught him completely by surprise, and his first essay at dram drinking ended in a prolonged and violent fit of coughing.

"You'll feel better for that," said MacWilliam, when the fit had subsided. "And now, Mr. Trimble, I owe you an apology."

The inspector shook his head. "I am sure, sir," he said faintly, when he was able to speak, "that you are entitled to do anything you think proper to—"

"I am not entitled to go behind the backs of members of my force in a criminal investigation. If I did it on this occasion it was for a particular reason. It won't occur again."

The inspector looked at the Chief Constable as though he were seeing him for the first time. In fact, it was the first time that he had ever been confident that his chief's words meant exactly what they said and nothing more.

"That is very generous of you, sir," he said.

MacWilliam had only one reply to remarks of this nature. "I am not a generous man," he said curtly. "It is a matter of simple justice."

"Perhaps at this point I should say something," Pettigrew observed. "Mr. MacWilliam thought fit to ask me, as a complete amateur, to consider the facts in this case, because he thought that my special knowledge might be of assistance in matters quite outside the ordinary run of police investigation. Well, I did what I was asked to do, and as a result I suggested a line of inquiry which has been carried out. The results of that inquiry have just come in and will, I have no doubt, be put before you as the officer in charge of the case"—he looked towards the Chief Constable, who nodded emphatic agreement—"for you to take such action on them as you may think proper. But I am bound to give it to you as my personal opinion—as I have just been giving it to the Chief Constable—that the knowledge so obtained is completely and absolutely useless. It is interesting in itself, perhaps, but it wholly fails to solve the problem presented by this case. That, Inspector, is what you might expect from calling in an amateur; and speaking for myself, I can heartily endorse what Mr. MacWilliam has just said—it won't occur again. And now," he concluded, rising to his feet, "I gather that you have something of importance to discuss. I shall only be in the way, so I will say good night."

Before MacWilliam could say anything Trimble interposed: "I'd rather you stayed, sir, if you don't mind. This case has given me a great deal of trouble, and what I came to tell the Chief Constable this evening seems to me to make it more difficult than ever. I—I'm a bit out of my depth, sir, and that's a fact. I had it at the back of my mind to ask the Chief to call in the Yard, but since you are here, perhaps you'll be able to save us from doing that. I thought I could run this show on my own, but it seems I can't, so I shall be glad of all the help I can get, and if you can give me a hand I shall be grateful."

Probably nobody but Trimble himself could have told just how much this avowal had cost him, but Pettigrew was sufficiently aware of the position to find the appeal irresistible.

"Of course I shall stay, if the Chief Constable will allow me," he said. "I have already given you my opinion on the value of amateur detection, so you have been warned." He settled down again in his chair, refused the whisky which MacWilliam immediately pressed upon him, and prepared to listen.

"Well, Inspector," said the Chief Constable, reverting to his official manner, "I understand you have a report to make to me."

"Not a report exactly, sir," said Trimble. "That is, I haven't had time to put the whole of it into writing. But in view of the importance of the matter I thought it best to bring it to your notice at once. You will have had the reports and statements dealing with this case up to yesterday, so you will be aware of the state of the inquiries to date."

"The last report before me covers your second interview with Mr. Ventry," said MacWilliam.

"Precisely, sir. Well, when I had reached that point I found myself fairly at a dead end. It seemed to me that I had pursued every line about as far as it would go, and I couldn't see which way to turn. That being so, with the assistance of Sergeant Tate" (here the inspector coughed in a somewhat self-conscious manner) "I went right through the whole case from the beginning, to see if there was anything that might have been missed. On rereading the papers, sir, it struck me that there was one witness whose evidence was in a marked degree unsatisfactory. I am referring, sir, to Mr. Clayton Evans."

"Clayton Evans, eh?" said MacWilliam. "This is very interesting, Mr. Trimble. Please go on."

"I would remind you, sir, of the second statement made by this witness. That statement contains a highly important disclosure as to the last time that Miss Carless was known to be alive, which he had entirely omitted from his first statement. His excuse for doing so was that he had not been asked for that particular piece of information in so many words, and when I suggested to him that this was an unreasonable attitude he went on to make a variety of wild and intemperate observations, sir, which you will find summarized in my report."

"I recollect them perfectly."

"Well, sir, it occurred to me that in view of Mr. Evans's rather exceptional approach to these matters there was quite a chance that he might still possess information of importance, which he had never bothered to disclose. So this evening I made an appointment with him and interviewed him for the third time. I decided to take no risks, but to question him precisely as to everything that had occurred within his recollection on the evening previous to and on the day of the concert. He displayed some considerable irritation during the course of the interview, sir, but I am bound to say that he answered my questions fairly, and his powers of memory appeared to be good. Nothing of importance transpired, however, until I reached the point in my examination where I was dealing with the scene that took place at the rehearsal as the result of which the Polish player retired from the orchestra. At this point, sir, Mr. Evans made a disclosure which seemed to me to be of first-class importance, so much so that I broke off the interview at once and came to consult you. I made a note of the relevant questions and answers immediately after the interview, sir, and though they are made from memory only, I think that they are approximately accurate."

The inspector here fished a notebook out of his waistcoat pocket and read as follows:

Question: After Zbartorowski had left the Hall in the way you have described, what did you do?

Answer: I have told you. I sent Dixon off to find another clarinet.

Question: What did you do next?

Answer: I told Miss Carless not to let this affair upset her and saw her off the platform.

Question: And then?

Answer: I then sent the orchestra back to their places and carried on.

Question: You mean you carried on with the rehearsal?

Answer: Of course.

Question: Was the rehearsal successful?

Answer: It was quite satisfactory.

Question: Although the orchestra was then deficient of one player?

Answer: It wasn't.

Question: But surely, you were then left with only one clarinet player instead of two?

Answer: I had no clarinets at all.

Question: I understood you to say that your orchestra contained two clarinets to start with?

Answer: That was the full orchestra. We had already rehearsed the Handel and the Mendelssohn concerto. All that was left to do was the symphony.

Question: Do you mean that it is possible to play a symphony without using clarinets?

Answer: Don't be silly. I am not talking about "a symphony," but this particular one.

Question: Very good, I should have said: Is it possible to play this particular symphony without using clarinets?

Answer: Really, I cannot go over the same ground continually. You already have the concert program. We were playing Mozart's symphony No. 38 in D, K.504, commonly called the Prague.

Question: I am aware of that. I am simply asking for a straight answer to this question: Do you use clarinets—

Answer: For goodness sake don't go on talking about "using" clarinets, as though they were toothpicks. The Prague symphony is not scored for clarinets. I imagined that everybody knew that.

The inspector looked up from his notebook.

"At this point, sir," he said, "Mr. Evans produced a large book of music, with some words on it in the German language, which he described as the score of the piece in question. I could not read it, of course, but he tendered it as evidence that clarinets are not employed in the symphony K.504. I then concluded my examination, as follows:

Question: At the concert was there not a full orchestra on the platform?

Answer: Certainly there was.

Question: But, as it turned out, the clarinets were not called upon to play?

Answer: Not except in the National Anthem.

Question: If the organ piece had been played first would the clarinets have been wanted?

Answer: Of course. We were using Henry Wood's arrangement. It is all in the program.

Inspector Trimble closed his notebook and put it away in his pocket.

"And what," said the Chief Constable after a long pause, "what is troubling you about this case now, Mr. Trimble?"

Trimble stared at him in surprise. "But don't you see, sir?" he said. "This means that the man we've been looking for all this time—this missing clarinetist—may not even have been a clarinetist at all. Nobody ever heard him play a note. He may have been just anybody. We've got to start all over again."

"On the contrary," said MacWilliam imperturbably. "Unless I am much mistaken, this is where we stop. Do you agree with me, Mr. Pettigrew?"

Pettigrew did not answer directly. His hands clasped round one knee, leaning back in his chair, he addressed nobody in particular.

"What a fool—what a doubly distilled idiot I have been!" he murmured. "The amateur all over! Here was this simple, obvious fact lying right under my nose—and I missed it. What did Evans say? 'I imagined that everybody knew that.' So they did—pretty nearly everybody connected with this case. Mrs. Basset knew it, Miss Porteous knew it. My own wife knew it perfectly well. I could have asked her at any time and got the simple answer. But it never occurred to me to ask, even when she offered to help me. This is a lesson to me, Inspector, to leave the business of detection to my betters."

Trimble cast a bewildered gaze from Pettigrew to MacWilliam and back again to Pettigrew.

"Do you mean, sir," he faltered, "that this piece of information actually helps the inquiry? When I heard it, I thought—"

"Helps!" exclaimed the Chief Constable. "Lord save us all! Here's a chiel who goes off on his own and solves the crime of the century, and he asks if it helps!" He poured out a bumper for himself and another for Pettigrew. "This deserves a drink if anything ever did. Mr. Trimble, your very good health! But where's your glass? Come now, I insist you should have a drop of something!"

"Thank you, sir," said the inspector faintly. "I'll have a small glass of soda water, if I may. And now, sir, perhaps you or Mr. Pettigrew wouldn't mind telling me just what I've done?"

19

Madam How and Lady Why

The Chief Constable looked across the room at Pettigrew.

"This is your show, I think," he said. "You tell him."

Pettigrew did not reply at once. "It's easy enough to say what you have done, Inspector," he said at last. "When I first propounded my theory to Mr. MacWilliam I told him that it led straight to an impossibility. We've been staring hopelessly at that impossibility ever since. You have removed it. That's all. So long as we were looking for a man who could play the clarinet we were looking for someone who simply did not exist. Now that we know we only have to find a man who could put on a false mustache and a pair of horn-rimmed spectacles and sit in the orchestra with a clarinet in his hand—well, there he is." He indicated with his hand the little bundle of official papers which the Chief Constable had produced to him earlier in the evening. "I should have explained," he added, "that I am alluding to my esteemed colleague, the secretary of the Markshire Orchestral Society."

"Mr. Dixon!" exclaimed Trimble. "Do you really mean Mr. Dixon, sir?"

"None other, I assure you. Assisted, I regret to have to say, by

Mrs. Dixon, who is on much better terms with her husband than she would have you believe."

"Mr. Dixon! But I don't understand. Why on earth should he have wanted to do such a thing?"

"As to the Why, that is where I come in. I spotted the Why some time ago, and the proof of it is in those papers over there. The really difficult problem was the How, and that you have succeeded in solving. With that done, it wouldn't have taken you very long to get at the truth, but as it is, I can shorten your labor. There are some details that are not quite clear to me at the moment, but I have no doubt you will be able to clear them up as we go along."

To look at Inspector Trimble at that moment, nobody would have believed that a short time before he had been on the verge of despair. With the complacent smile of success, he was sitting back to hear his assistant put the finishing touches to his work. Something very like a wink passed from MacWilliam to Pettigrew as the latter proceeded:

"Why? Why should Dixon wish to murder the woman from whom he was comfortably divorced as long ago as 1942? Both he and she had married again and they were as completely uninterested in each other's lives—or deaths—as any two people could possibly be, to all appearances. Oddly enough, though, the motive for Dixon wanting to get rid of his ex-wife was presented to me at a very early stage in the case, in fact more than twenty-four hours before it was a case for the police at all. The person who gave me the hint, quite unconsciously, was Lucy Carless herself. I don't know whether you are a reader of Dickens, Inspector?"

"I can't say I am, sir. I have tried him once or twice, but I found him a bit too wordy for me."

"Miss Carless had also tried Dickens—or rather he had been tried on her, with rather unfortunate results, it appeared. At Mr. Ventry's famous party I happened to raise the subject of Dickens with her, and mentioned *David Copperfield*."

"That's one of the ones I dipped into, sir. There was a fellow in it called Micawber, I recollect, who was very comical."

"Quite right. There were also two ladies who successively married the hero, named respectively Dora and Agnes."

"That Dora! I think that was the bit of the book where I got bogged."

"I can't altogether blame you. Miss Carless held similar, and even stronger, views about that character. Now the point is this: Dora, in the story, is a charming but not altogether satisfactory wife, who conveniently dies, leaving the hero free to marry the equally charming and entirely satisfactory Agnes. As a matter of history, Dickens's own marriage was somewhat of a failure, and he appears to have got it very firmly into his head that the girl he ought to have married was not his wife, but her younger sister. Whether things would have turned out any better if he had there is, of course, no knowing. But that being his state of mind, and since *David Copperfield* is obviously largely autobiographical, you can well imagine that many readers today identify Dora with Mrs. Dickens and Agnes with her sister—the convenient death of Dora and the subsequent marriage with Agnes being in the nature of what the psychoanalysts call 'wish-fulfillment.'"

"Very interesting, sir, but I don't quite see—"

"You will in a moment. As soon as ever I mentioned *David Copperfield* to Miss Carless she referred, not, as you very properly did, to Micawber, but to Dora and Agnes and to the commonplace identification of them with Dickens's wife and sister-in-law. And she followed it up with these words—I think that I can recollect them exactly: 'What a fuss he made about it! Nowadays he'd have simply got a divorce and married the other one!' It struck me at the time that she seemed to be taking rather a strong personal interest in what is, after all, fairly ancient history, and I puzzled over it a good deal. Later on, a simple explanation occurred to me, which has now turned out to be the true one. Miss Carless was identifying herself with Dora—or with Mrs. Dickens, if you prefer

190

it—and Dixon had done exactly what she suggested Dickens might have done."

"With Mrs. Dixon, that now is, standing for Agnes?"

"Exactly."

"But surely, sir, the two ladies weren't sisters? Miss Carless's father was a Polish count and Mrs. Dixon's maiden name was Minch—or so Mrs. Basset says."

"What Mrs. Basset says *Debrett* also says, and both are correct. What neither of them say, but is none the less true, is that Mrs. Minch and the Countess Carlessoff (or should it be Carlessova?) were one and the same person. Mrs. Dixon that was, and Mrs. Dixon that is, were half sisters."

"You still haven't told me, sir," Trimble reminded Pettigrew, "why Dixon should have wanted to kill Miss Carless."

"I thought I had made it clear. It was so that he could marry her sister."

"Marry her? But isn't that just what he'd done, years ago?"

"He had gone through a form of marriage with her, certainly. The Chief Constable has the certificate in front of him at this moment. But it is of no legal effect whatever. You may not lawfully marry your divorced wife's sister—and a half sister, for this purpose, counts as a full one. That is the result of an Act of Parliament passed in the reign of Henry VIII—a gentleman who knew quite a bit about divorces. On the other hand, modern legislation has made it possible to marry a deceased wife's sister, and that is exactly what Dixon intended to do."

Seeing the look of incredulity on Trimble's face, Pettigrew added: "Just to prove that this is not a piece of guesswork on my part, you will find on that table Dixon's application to the ecclesiastical official known as the Surrogate, asking for the issue of a marriage license to enable him to marry Nicola Minch, spinster. It is dated just a week after Lucy Carless's death. The license, of course, would enable him to marry without the publicity of banns, or giving notice at a register office."

The inspector was still only half convinced.

"What beats me about the whole business is this," he said. "Here's a man in a good position, who, so far as anyone can tell, is comfortably married—he *is* married, to all intents and purposes, whatever the law may say. Why on earth should he run the fearful risk of committing a murder just to put himself right with the letter of the law, when he could have gone on as he was, and nobody any the wiser?"

"Because," said Pettigrew, "he found himself in a position where he had to put himself right with the law, or sooner or later a great many people would be the wiser. Two unexpected events occurred just before the concert. The first was the death of the only son of Lord Simonsbath. That, as anybody within earshot of Mrs. Basset must have heard, left Dixon the next heir to the peerage, though his succession was liable to be defeated by the birth of a posthumous son to the widow. Then the posthumous child duly appeared and proved to be a girl. After that, whether he liked it or not, nothing but a miracle could prevent Dixon becoming the seventh Viscount, and, again according to the omniscient Mrs. Basset, the present peer is a pretty poor life, so that it might occur at any time."

Pettigrew paused for a moment.

"Here," he said, "I am obliged to speculate a little, but from what we now know happened I think I am on fairly safe ground. Whether married or living in sin, Dixon would unquestionably be Lord Simonsbath, and I don't suppose anyone would question Mrs. Dixon's right to call herself My Lady. But suppose he wanted to set up a family himself? Suppose—and time will very soon show if I am right—she is already in what the newspapers call 'a certain condition'? I don't profess to be an expert in such matters, but I fancy that before anyone can succeed to a peerage he has to take some steps to prove his right to do so. There would be a pretty kettle of fish, would there not, when Dixon's son came to man's estate and it turned out that after all he was what the law crudely styles a bastard. Plain Mr. Dixon could afford to let things go on in the way they always had done. Lord Simonsbath simply could not—and even if he was prepared to, the lady who had always passed as his wife was not going to let him."

"When I was a boy," observed the Chief Constable, "I was given a damned dull book to read. I've forgotten most of it, but the title has always stuck in my head. It was *Madam How and Lady Why*. It seems appropriate to this case, somehow."

"I think we have disposed of Lady Why," said Pettigrew, "and I must apologize for letting her ladyship take up so much of your time. And now, Inspector, we are waiting for you to give us Madam How."

Inspector Trimble drew a deep breath. From the very beginning of the investigation he had been looking forward to the moment when before an admiring audience (which would certainly include the Chief Constable) he would demonstrate with telling logic and crystalline clarity the solution to the problem. Since then his confidence had wavered until, less than an hour ago, it had reached vanishing point. Now, it seemed, when he was least expecting it, his hour had struck. He was a successful detective after all! Except for one little detail—which, as Mr. Pettigrew pointed out, he would have found out for himself in due course—he had unraveled the mystery; and here was his audience, waiting breathless on his words. He could have wished for a little more time to assemble his thoughts—to assimilate the little detail which, he recognized, was not without its importance. But he would do his best. Tentatively at first, and then with growing assurance, he began his exposition.

"It's a bit of a jigsaw puzzle, sir," he said, "but I think that I can explain how it fits together. Let's start at the beginning: Dixon made up his mind to kill Miss Carless in the artist's room at the concert. In order to do that he had to impersonate a member of the orchestra, relying on the fact that players in an orchestra don't look at each other during a performance but at the conductor, and the conductor in this case was as blind as a bat. The trouble was that he couldn't play a note himself. But he noticed that one of the pieces to be played—this K. thing—didn't use clarinets, and he decided that he would pretend to be a clarinet player for the occasion. As I see it he had three difficulties to get over before he could bring it off: One, to get hold of a clarinet; Two, to get rid of the genuine player; Three, to arrange for this K. affair to be played at the start of the concert, instead of at the end, as arranged. Am I right so far, sir?"

"In my humble opinion, absolutely right," said Pettigrew.

"The first job was easy enough. I take it that he simply lifted Mr. Ventry's instrument at the party. The second must have given him a bit of trouble, though. But luckily for him he was able to take advantage of the row that blew up at the rehearsal between Miss Carless and the Polish fellow."

"There I am afraid I must disagree with you," said Pettigrew. "There was no luck in the matter at all. The whole affair was deliberately staged by Dixon."

"Are you sure of that, sir?"

"Looking back on the occasion—and don't forget that I was an eyewitness—I have no doubt about it whatever. It seemed to me at the time that Dixon was showing an extraordinary lack of tact in dragging Zbartorowski up to be presented to the soloist. He was obviously reluctant to be brought forward and only wanted to be left alone. Introducing him to Miss Carless was like introducing a spark to a powder barrel."

"How did he know that?"

"How was he not to know it? Dixon had lived in Poland. He had been given the job of vetting Zbartorowski before Evans would admit him to the orchestra. Of course he had found out all about him, and knew that if there was one name calculated to send Lucy off the handle it was his."

"Very good, sir. Having got rid of one player in this way, of course he was given the job of finding another one. As we know, he eventually succeeded in engaging Mr. Jenkinson."

"Here again I think I can help you. It is a lamentable fact, but I have just realized that I am going to be an important witness for the prosecution. Dixon wasted a considerable amount of time, no doubt deliberately, in trying a number of different people before he finally pitched on Jenkinson, whom he must have known to be available all along. I think this was done so that it would be too late for him to come direct to Markhampton, which was essential to his plan. Also you will note that he so arranged matters that I and not he made the first contact with Jenkinson, by way of additional proof, if necessary, that the man had been genuinely engaged. Incidentally, Evans very nearly queered his pitch at the last moment by offering to do without a clarinetist, but luckily for him the offer came just too late."

"That is very helpful, sir." The inspector's tone, to MacWilliam's disguised amusement, had become positively patronizing. "Now we come to an odd point: Dixon then and there, in the presence of you and a number of other people, purported to ring up Farren's garage for a car to meet the seven twenty-nine train at Eastbury Junction. But Farren is positive that the message he received was to meet the seven fifty-nine train. Moreover, he says that the message came at five twenty, whereas Mrs. Basset is prepared to swear that Dixon telephoned in her presence at five ten. Up to now I've gone on the line that either Farren or Mrs. Basset or both were mistaken. It looks now as if they were right. Somebody did, later on, tell Farren to meet the wrong train. That, of course, must have been Dixon. The message which you heard Mr. Dixon send, sir, must have been a fake, sent to some other number on the Markhampton exchange."

"By Jove!" said Pettigrew.

"What is it, sir?"

"I have just remembered something. Not only was the message a fake, but it was spotted as such by one of those present at the time it was made, even though he did not realize the effect of his own observation."

"You spotted it at the time, sir?"

"Not I—but Clayton Evans certainly did. If you had got so far in your last interview with him he might have told you. Let me

195

recall exactly what occurred. Dixon said: 'I am going to ring up Farren's,' or words to that effect. (He had let me do the telephoning up to then, of course, but this time he was careful to do it himself.) He then repeated the number—2203—and proceeded to dial. But of course he didn't dial that number, but another one. We shall see in a moment which that number really was. Now if you listen to a number being dialed on an automatic telephone you can tell, if you are sufficiently interested to notice, whether the digits composing the number are long or short by the time taken for the dial to come back to its position. Obviously our old friend 999 would take much longer to dial than 111, for instance. If you have a very keen and observant ear trained to notice exact gradations of speed, I dare say you could tell the difference, say, between dialing 99 and 98. Of course, I haven't an ear like that— but Evans certainly has. Well, as he left the room just after the bogus telephone call had been made I noticed that he looked distinctly puzzled. Somebody asked him if anything was the matter, and he said that something had been bothering him—he wasn't quite sure what, but he thought it was a question of *tempo*. Of course it was. He had been expecting to hear Dixon dial 2203 and what he had heard in fact was the sound of dialing 2381. Without realizing it consciously he felt that something was wrong with the timing and it upset him, just as an orchestra playing out of time would have done."

"2381," said the Chief Constable. "That is Dixon's own telephone number, is it not?"

"Yes. There is only one person to whom he could have possibly given that fake message and that was his wife—as it is convenient to call her. We aren't in a position to prove it, of course, but if Ventry is asked I shall be surprised if he doesn't say that a telephone call came through to her at ten minutes past five."

"Ventry," repeated the inspector, who obviously felt that he had been kept from the center of the stage quite long enough. "I was just coming to him. Dixon had still his third hurdle to get over—he had to prevent the items at the concert being played in their proper order. The obvious way to do that was to arrange for Ventry to turn up late at the concert, and rely on Mr. Evans's anxiety not to keep the audience waiting. Well, we know where Ventry was, all right. He was having what he calls 'fun and games' with Mrs. Dixon. She, no doubt, had told him that the coast would be clear that afternoon and early evening—Yes?" he broke off impatiently, as Pettigrew showed signs of speaking again.

"I am sorry to butt in once more," said Pettigrew humbly, "but I am a witness of fact on that point also. Dixon made it very clear to me, in Ventry's hearing, that he would not be coming home between the concert and the rehearsal. When the shemozzle over finding another clarinetist began Ventry weighed in with the suggestion that Clarkson should be approached. Dixon fairly bit his head off, and thereupon Ventry beetled away with what I now recognize to have been a 'You Have Been Warned' expression on his face."

"Thank you, sir," said Trimble graciously. "Dixon and his wife between them baited the trap and Ventry fell into it. Once at the house, it was her business to keep him there. She was able to do that by setting her clock twenty minutes slow and only leaving the house just in time to drive down to the concert before it was due to begin. Ventry followed her out, and found that his own car was gone."

"On the whole," said MacWilliam, "I think that was the most ingenious part of the entire scheme. Dixon had to ditch Ventry. At the same time he wanted a car to meet Jenkinson's train and ditch him. He killed two birds with one stone in the simplest possible fashion, by taking Ventry's car and using it to get Jenkinson out of the way. I am bound to say I rather admire him for thinking of that."

"At the same time," Trimble went on, "he was throwing suspicion on Ventry, who was naturally reluctant to tell the truth about his adventures that evening. The rest of the story is quite straightforward. Dixon drove to Eastbury Junction, met Mr. Jenkinson there, landed him at Didford Parva and then came back to

Markhampton, timing himself to arrive just as the concert was due to begin. He entered the Hall by the artists' entrance. By that time, of course, the back of the Hall was deserted, as the orchestra was all assembled on the platform. While the National Anthem was being played he made his way into the soloist's room and strangled Miss Carless with one of his wife's nylon stockings, which he had brought with him. Presumably he was successful in taking her by surprise, but if there was any struggle the sound of it would be drowned by the noise of the music. Then he slipped into his place in the orchestra and sat there quietly, in full view of the audience, while the symphony was being played. In the confusion that followed the discovery of the crime it was quite easy for him to slip out, remove his very simple disguise and reappear in his ordinary capacity as secretary to the Society. Naturally, nobody thought of asking him where he had been that evening," the inspector added defensively. "As secretary he would, of course, be expected to be here, there and everywhere up to the time of the concert and to have a seat somewhere in the hall while it was going on."

"Exactly," said Pettigrew. He was recollecting how he had sat in the gallery of the City Hall, and chatted amiably with the accomplice of a murderer, while she airily explained that her husband "had a seat downstairs, somewhere near the back"; how he had eagerly looked along the rows of musicians and seen their ranks joined by the very murderer himself fresh from his crime. His mind reverted again to Nicola Dixon. How sparkling and alive she had been! As he contemplated the real causes of her eager excitement on that evening, he shuddered.

Aloud he said: "I congratulate you, Inspector. It has been a most complicated affair, but your reconstruction of it appears to me perfect."

"Thank you, sir," said Trimble modestly. "I think it is pretty clear now. And, if I may say so, your assistance has been most valuable."

The Chief Constable choked over his fifth whisky and soda.

20

Da Capo

"I call upon the secretary," said Mrs. Basset in her high, neighing voice, "to read the minutes of the last meeting."

In his time Francis Pettigrew had aspired to, and even applied for, a number of appointments of different kinds. He had, in fact, held not a few, most of them honorary. But the last job that he had ever expected to come his way was that of honorary secretary to the Markshire Orchestral Society. None the less, fate and the operation of law had between them created a gap which he had had no option but to fill. With deep distaste he opened the book and read from the late secretary's neat script: "At a meeting held at Mrs. Basset's house on the 15th of July ..."